I0611383

ASSEMBLE THE PARTY

ANTONY SOEHNER

5 PRINCE PUBLISHING

Published by 5 PRINCE PUBLISHING & BOOKS, LLC PO Box 865, Arvada, CO 80001

www.5PrinceBooks.com

ISBN digital: 978-1-63112-234-7

ISBN print: 978-1-63112-235-4

Cover Credit: Joshua Stolte

To Papa,
This wouldn't be possible without you.
Be careful

ACKNOWLEDGMENTS

To my friends and family for their love and support.

And to my friend Josh without whom these stories would never have come alive!

ALSO BY ANTONY SOEHNER

Gather the Party

Unite the Party

Assemble the Party

ASSEMBLE THE PARTY

ANTONY SOEHNER

TALES OF 1504 CEDARMEN DRIVE

THIS WAS A TYPICAL FRIDAY NIGHT DRIVE. FULL FOCUS ON the road ahead and preparing myself for tonight's game. Rain littered my windshield, but there wasn't quite enough falling to get my wipers wet. They squeaked across the semi-dry glass every time I pushed the bar up to set them off. Occasionally I pulled it towards me to use the wiper fluid to get the glass wet enough to not ruin my blades.

The song *Let's Go Crazy* by Prince came on and I bobbed my head with the song's drum beat. This song always put me in a great mood. And lately, that mood had been sticking around.

Things were going pretty good for us. Mom had saved up enough money, after being promoted at the bar and her finally being okay with using Dad's life insurance, that she was able to negotiate a deal with the previous owners when they were selling the place. She is now the proud owner of Travis' Bar. She managed to work it into a more family-friendly place and hired Liam, Ben, Daryl, and I. She also got Laura into some bartending classes, making her head chef and weekend bartender. Jake swings by and helps us out every once in a while, when he's not working.

Mom created this business with our ragtag family of misfits, wackadoos, and what-cha-ma-call-its. Mr. R even comes by on nights Liam works and hangs out at the bar with Jake. It's become a new hangout for us.

But that hasn't changed our Friday night routine. We still all get together at Mr. R's house for game night. Mom has a whole Friday night staff. A group of employees who work throughout the week with us when Mom schedules them, but they're all on the schedule for Friday nights so that the seven of us can play.

I took a deep breath, letting it fill my chest before slowly exhaling. "Adrik Frostbeard," I started to recite out loud. "Level sixteen dwarf barbarian. A hundred and seventy hit points. Nineteen strength," A smile grew across my face like it always did. "Ten charisma."

It had finally happened last week! We'd been searching for weeks now since Greg disappeared, and I had just leveled up again. I finally got to move my charisma score to ten! I no longer had any negative modifiers, and boy, did it feel great.

I pulled up in front of Liam's house, and of course, I was first. Wouldn't be right any other way. But when I put my car in park and the song faded out, a car pulled up behind me with music blasting so loud I could hear the song as if I was playing it in my car. It was *Enjoy the Rain* by Good Tiger, and that could only mean one thing.

"Laura," I mumbled under my breath. I could already feel my legs wobbling and I hadn't even stood up. I began to struggle to breathe, like my seatbelt had tightened against my chest. I quickly unbuckled and opened my center console. I reached inside and grabbed my inhaler and gave it two quick puffs.

There was a knock on my window. I jumped, dropping my inhaler on the floor. I turned to see Ben and Laura with their faces pressed against my window. Ben had his mouth open showing me his entire mouth. Laura had her nose flattened in a pig snout look. I rolled my eyes and smiled at the two. "It's like you're related." I mouthed to the brother, sister comedy duo in my window. I rolled down the window and they both backed up.

"Did we scare ya?" Ben asked. His eyes moving to the floor of my car.

I reached down and picked up my inhaler. "No," I lied. "You know my mom always wants me to bring this with me. I was just pulling it out to put in my bag."

"Whatever you say, wheezy." He mocked as he walked off towards the front door.

In response, I shot my middle finger straight up. He shot me finger guns and continued walking.

"Ignore him." Laura laughed.

I turned to face her, and there was that beautiful complexion sitting in front of me. I froze in my seat. She was really close, like noses-almost-touching close.

I never know how to read these situations. I've spent years trying to figure women out. All these girls my age like to flirt and tell me about how great I'd be as a boyfriend, some even come hang out at my house and watch movies with me. But whenever I think about asking them out or asking what we are, they all freak out on me, telling me I'm the same scumbag guy as the rest. But Laura has always been different. She didn't flirt around with me. Heck, we don't hang out more than at work and on Fridays. But seriously, I think she might be the one. There's still that stupid age barrier though.

"You okay?" she asked.

I blinked back into reality. "W-what?" I stuttered. "Oh, yeah! Just got lost—"

"In my eyes?" She finished my thought for me. "You need a better excuse, dude. You use that every time you zone out looking at me."

"I-I—," I tried to answer. But I had nothing.

"It's cool." She laughed. "I know they're a soul-sucking pool. You don't have to be nice about it."

"Heh-heh," I fake laughed. I wasn't going to agree to that. Everything about her was perfect. Her smile that spreads to her gorgeous eyes, the Metallica tank top under the Star Wars replica jacket, and the custom sneakers she'd painted with The Flash all over them. She was a walking billboard of geek, and I loved it!

"Jack?" She snapped her fingers in my face. "Dude, what is it? You okay today?"

"Yeah," I responded. "I just love you—" I caught myself. "Your presence!" I could feel my heart racing again and the blood rushing to my face. My eyes felt like they were bulging. That was not slick at all! How stupid was I? How could you say that to her? You're not even dating! She's still too old for you! What the—

She leaned in, though the car window, and kissed my lips. I could feel my legs tense up in panic for a moment. She pulled away and chuckled.

"You're such a dork, Jack." She smiled at me. She tousled

my hair. "Are you gonna be alright in there tonight? We have a world to save and I can't have you distracted!"

I nodded.

"Actually," I blurted out. What am I doing? This isn't going to work! Don't do it, you idiot! Don't do it!

But I did. I put my hand on her cheek and pulled her in for another kiss. A long one. My whole body felt like it melted in my seat.

Had that actually worked? Not only is she not pulling away, but she's kissing me back still.

"Oh good Lord Pelor above!" A voice broke in.

I scrambled towards the origin of the voice to find Liam now sitting in my passenger seat.

"Would you two get a room, please?" He asked. He then proceeded to fake gag.

"Would you mind your own business?" I scolded him. "Laura and I were having a private conversation!"

"People usually talk with their tongues in their own mouths you know," He laughed as he swung out of the car, bouncing it as he did. "So whenever you two are done swapping spit, we'd love to have you inside."

He ran back towards the house as I gave him the same gesture I gave Ben.

"Alright Casanova," Laura smiled at me. "Let's go before they get suspicious."

I grabbed her jacket and pulled her in for one more quick kiss before she turned and walked towards the house.

What in the world just happened? Did I just make out with Laura? My dream girl? This has to be a dream! I reached down and pinched my leg.

Nope, not a dream. This was really happening! Laura is

actually into me! Me! How was that possible? In every book and movie I've seen or read, the guy like me doesn't get the girl! It's not a thing!

I've dreamt that this would happen one day, but I couldn't have imagined it anytime soon. I'm always much older in my mind. Something of a rom-com kind of story. Guy she's with breaks her heart, best friend and true love; me, swoops in, reminds her how amazing and beautiful she is. Get married and grow old together, live a long, happy and geeky life together—

"Dude!" I heard Liam's voice again coming from my passenger side. Followed with a smack on the back side of my head.

"Ow!" I cried out.

"Seriously are you done gawking at her? She's not even standing there anymore." Liam reminded me.

"I wasn't gawking!" I lied. "I was getting in my pre-game headspace."

"No you weren't." He rolled his eyes. "You had that stupid smile on your face that you always get when you're daydreaming about your cheesy romantic comedy fantasy. The one where you and Laura grow old together."

"I don't know what you're talking about," I denied.

"Yes you do." He elbowed my side. "Where some guy breaks her heart, you swoop in and save—"

"Not a clue," I lied again.

"Whatever you say, Mr. Sparks. Whatever you say." He closed the car door and walked back towards the house again. "Let's go."

I killed the engine, unplugged my phone, and walked to the back of the car. Opening the back and grabbing my bag out, I threw it over my shoulder and closed the door. Clicking the key fob, the car locked with a beep and I made my way inside. Stepping into the house I could hear two cars pulling onto the gravel drive.

"Hey Liam," I shouted into the house. "Wade is here! You got the pizza money?"

"Don't worry about it!" I heard a voice call from outside. "We got it!"

I turned to see Daryl and Jake walking up the walkway with pizzas and a grocery bag.

"Wasn't Wade this time," Jake said. "New kid. Probably a week or two into working there."

"Is Wade okay?" I asked.

"Yeah said Wade's okay. Just running the shop tonight," Daryl answered.

I eyed him before reaching into my pocket and pulling my phone out. I clicked it open and went to my favorite contacts. Clicking on the contact 'Pizza'.

"What're you doing?" Daryl asked.

I held my finger up to him. The phone rang twice before a familiar voice answered.

"Kurtis' pizzeria and delicatessen. Wade speaking. How may I help you on this bodacious Friday evening?" Wade recited.

"Wade!" I said into the phone. "Hey, it's Jack!"

Before I could continue he spoke up, "Hey Jack-attack! What's going on my dude! Did y'all get your pizzas?"

"Yeah, we just did," I assured him. "I was calling to check and make sure everything was okay. The new guy said you were running the shop tonight."

"Oh yeah, I had to send out Tal tonight." He sighed. "Kurtis had a bit of a health scare yesterday. Ashley walked into the shop and found him passed out in the kitchen. Doc says he was overworking himself. Prescribed some medical stuff and some well-needed time off."

"But he's gonna be okay?" I asked.

"Oh for sure, bud." Wade chuckled. "He's a-okay! He came in a little bit ago to make sure you guys got your order in even."

"Well, we're glad he's okay. Let him know we can't wait to hear from him when he's back."

"Will do, my man. Will diddly do," Wade sang. "You dudes have a fun night. Good luck on that Greg adventure."

"Thanks, Wade, take it easy," I told him.

"You too, Jack. Peace!" The line went silent before the phone clicked telling me he hung up.

"What's up?" Jake asked.

"Wade's running the shop tonight. Said Kurtis was told to take some time off. Doctor's orders," I explained.

"Well, as long as he's okay." Daryl sighed in relief.

"You said it." Jake laughed. "That man's been throwing pizza since I was little. Couldn't imagine that place when he's gone."

"Well, let's not think about it," I said. "By the sounds of it, we won't have to worry about it for a while longer."

"Here's the money!" Liam ran into the room.

"You're too late," Jake chuckled. "We got it already."

"What?" Liam stood there in disappointment. "I didn't even get to say hi to Wade!"

"Well none of us did," I shrugged. "He's running the store tonight while Kurtis is out."

"Is he okay?" Liam's eyes grew wider.

"He's fine," I explained again. "Just needed a little vacation."

"Let's get these bad boys into the kitchen," Jake said patting the pizza boxes in his arms.

We all marched our way into the kitchen. And per usual with our group of friends, Laura and Ben had their Gameboys out. Connected between them was a semi-transparent cable.

"I've got Hitmonlee. Trade him for your Scyther?" Ben negotiated.

Laura swished her cheeks back and forth. "How about Hitmonlee for Jigglypuff? Or my Scyther for your Moltres. That would complete my legendary set."

"Hey!" Daryl interrupted the negotiation table. "Those are both mine!"

"It's just for Pokedex stats," Ben defended. "They'll go back to you. We're just trading around to complete our dex."

"Give you my second Mew to keep him." Laura smiled.

"Like I need another. I already have all of theirs," Daryl laughed as he gestured to the rest of us.

"Well then why would you need either of these back?" Ben asked.

"Because I'm a perfectionist," Daryl smirked. "What's the point of being the very best if you don't have the very best?"

"I have no words." Laura scrunched her face.

"I'll battle you to win them back!" Ben challenged.

"You think that's going to go well for you?" Daryl folded his arms and shifted his weight to his back leg.

"I think it'd be worth the shot," Ben replied. He was chewing the inside of his cheek. A dead giveaway that he's nervous.

Daryl swung his bag around and opened it. He threw his hand deep into the bag before pulling out his own Gameboy.

"You really think you're ready for this?" Daryl asked.

Ben looked back at his Gameboy before looking back at Daryl, an ominous grin across his face. He said nothing and just nodded at Daryl. He offered him the other end of the cable that was connected to Laura's Gameboy.

I pushed my way around the dueling nitwits and grabbed myself a plate and some pizza. I scooted to the fridge and grabbed a root beer before heading into the game room out of all the chaos.

"Take that, son!" I heard Ben shout as I passed into the room.

I went to my seat and set my food on the table. Dropped my bag and placed it on the chair. I reached inside and pulled out the binder and player's handbook, setting them next to my plate. Reaching back into my bag, I pulled out my dice bag, and dropped it on my books with a thud and a rattle.

"Hey! Just the man I was looking for."

I spun around to see Mr. R sitting in the doorway. He wheeled his way over to me and handed me a folded piece of paper.

"What's this?" I asked him. I could feel my eyebrow arching.

"Open it and see." He smiled at me, pushing the paper closer to me.

I took it from him and opened it. Inside was a picture. Mom in a hospital gown. In her arms was a baby. I was that baby. But behind my mother and I, was my dad passed out in the hospital bed. And behind him, a standing, younger Mr. R with a cup of water pouring out on my dad.

I couldn't help but let out a laugh. This was an amazing picture!

"Where did you get this?" I asked. The smile on my face never dropping.

"It was in a stash of Marisha's things I found in the basement." He said. You could see the physical battle on his face to avoid any outward sign of pain. "It was in the box of the undeveloped film she had. Figured it was time to sort through her things. I took her box of film to Walgreens and got them developed. This was the first picture I pulled out when I got home."

"Tell me you printed doubles?" I shook my head laughing. There was a knot forming in my throat. "You need to always have a copy of this picture." I croaked out through the knot.

"Oh, I've got one. Don't you worry." He assured me. "A genuine moment like this. I couldn't pass up my own copy!"

"Mom's gonna love this! Thanks, Mr. R." I leaned over and gave him a hug. When I rested my chin on his shoulder, I caught a glimpse at a box sitting on the floor behind him. It was labeled—

Marisha's Things
Box 3 of 20

On top of the box were some cameras. There was a Polaroid camera sitting next to an older film camera. And next to that was a large, professional, digital camera.

"Are those her cameras?" I asked, standing back up and moving towards them to get a closer look.

"That's her collection." He sighed. "Her work camera, art camera, and spur of the moment camera. She sure did take a lot of pictures. That box could tell a bazillion stories."

I picked up the film camera and saw there were still unused frames on the counter. There was a roll still in there. I advanced the film to load the next frame, turned to Mr. R and said, "Smile!"

The camera shutter clicked. I advanced the film again and hung the camera around my neck.

"Do you mind if I use these tonight?"

"By all means, kiddo." He smiled. "They're all yours. She was your aunt after all."

I couldn't believe it. After all these years, I owned Aunt Marisha's cameras. They were mine. I also couldn't believe that he was willing to part with them. Ninety percent of these undeveloped film cartridges were probably shots of him.

"I have a feeling that wherever your dad and she are right now, they're smiling bright," Mr. R said, choking through the tears now welling in his eyes. "Now why don't we stop getting emotional over the past and go gather everyone together? Get this game a-rollin'."

THE KING AND US

Mr. R wheeled further into the game room from the kitchen doorway, followed by everyone else. Ben walked in last with his head hung low.

"How?" he muttered under his breath.

"Yo, Jack!" Jake shouted across the room. "Where'd you get the fancy new gear?" he asked pointing at the camera around my neck.

I looked down at the camera and then back at Jake. "It was my aunt's. Mr. R gave it to me." I picked up the camera and aimed it at Jake. The camera's shutter clicked. I advanced the film for the next shot. "I figured what would be better to carry on her legacy than candid shots at a D&D game?"

"I love it!" Jake laughed.

Everyone made their way to their seats and began their pregame rituals. Daryl sorted through his already sorted dice box. Liam trained his dice. Laura put in her color-changing contact lenses.

Mr. R cleared his throat. "Alright," he said before clicking his tongue in thought. "Let's get this started. Mr. Adrik Frost-beard. How are you this rainy evening?"

"Yar!" I cheered. "Ready to smash some skulls together!"

"And Ront, how about you?" Mr. R motioned to his nephew.

"Hmpf," Liam exhaled. "Another day of life, another day of adventuring."

"Rolen?" Mr. R turned his hand towards Ben.

"Nature shall guide me to finding Elfi and ending Greg once and for all."

"May the elements have mercy," Mr. R nodded. "Torinn."

"Oh yes," Daryl coughed out. "May the light of Pelor guide us through the tunnel of this adventure."

"Keep those eyes open. Lerissa?"

"Let's find Greg and end him finally! His time is well over-due," Laura answered.

"That it is. And Gimble," Mr. R turned to face Jake.

"I hope to keep the inspiration high, and the laughter loud," Jake announced.

"Very good." Mr. R clapped his hands together and gave them a rub back and forth. "You six have been in search of the necromancer and aspiring lich, Greg, for months now. Traversing the world. Searching high and low. From the monasteries high in the mountains to the underground market of Shadestone, you have come close to finding him. But still, nothing. You now find yourselves in the heart of the Shadestone underground watching Adrik as he fights for his life in an illegal gladiatorial ring." Mr. R clicked on the keyboard, his laptop already plugged in and set up. The black screen in the table suddenly showed an image of an ancient Roman gladiatorial ring. "You hear a voice ring across the stadium." He clicked his keyboard again and an uproar of cheers and screams rang out from the speakers. "Subjects! This man was found stealing, forcing himself upon a woman, and killing innocent beings of our sovereign city—"

"Lies!" I snarled back.

"And now interrupting the crown!" The voice continued. "What do you think, my subjects? Shall we introduce this scum to Thray'dar?"

The volume of the cheering increased. The water in Daryl's glass began to ripple.

"You think I'm afraid?" I taunted. "Bring it on!" I threw my arms out wide.

"On the far side of the ring from you, Adrik, the rusted iron rod gate begins to slowly click its way down into the ground." Mr. R tapped his keyboard and the clicking sounds began. "And then from deep inside the tunnel, an echoing roar rips through the stadium." He clicked again and the gate sound stopped. Followed by another click. The echoing roar reminded me of the Tyrannosaurus Rex from Jurassic Park.

"I grip my berserker axe tightly," I said.

"You feel a surge of rage begin to rush into your chest from the axe, overpowering any fear that lingered," Mr. R described.

I took a large gulp and picked up my d20.

"Ladies and gentlemen!" The voice boomed again. "I present your reigning champion! Thray'dar!" The roaring got louder and the cheering became thunderous. "From the open gateway across the ring, a spark of blue lightning blasts out, illuminating the tunnel. In the tunnel, a large humanoid figure lingers. It steps out into the light." Mr. R clicked his keyboard.

On the screen, a blue dragonborn appeared on the image of

the fighting ring. The dragonborn wore very little, an elegant loincloth trimmed with gold, its right arm plated with thick golden armor. In its hand is a scimitar that it drags behind itself. The other arm is hidden behind a shield, and from that hand, a metal net drapes to the floor.

I sat up in my chair, rolling my shoulders back and popping my neck. I folded my fingers together and gave them a nice crack. "I am Adrik Frostbeard," I growled, letting it ring through the room. "And I am the last being you shall ever cross blades with!"

"Roll initiative," Mr. R said.

I opened my dice bag and picked my pink d20 out of the inside pocket. I shook it before dropping it on the table. I rolled a second time for my initiative advantage. I scrunched up my face. "Seven."

"Alright," Mr. R nodded. "As you threaten the mighty dragonborn before you, what you could almost distinguish as a smile curls across his leathery face. The fighter shifts their stance drops their shield and points the scimitar at you. They drop the net atop the shield and with the now empty hand, the dragonborn grabs the scimitar. And like magic, the scimitar splits in two separate swords. One in each hand." He clicked the keyboard and the image shifted to the dual weapon-wielding dragonborn. "They drop an arm at their side, and point a scimitar at the ground where the shield and net lay. They open their mouth. Sparks of blue static begin to form in their maw!"

"Oh—Fudge," I rolled out slowly.

"Roll me a dexterity saving throw," Mr. R said.

I winced at my two rolls. "Three."

"In a moment that feels like it lasts forever, the blue static begins to hop from the fighter's snout, circulate the extended arm, gleam across the surface of the scimitar all the way to the tip before exploding outwards at you., blasting your chest and knocking you backward and prone."

"Shocking!" Ront laughed.

"You take..." Mr. R rolled behind his screen. "Nine lightning damage."

I whistled a descending tone shaking my head as if I were clearing my thoughts. "Looks like you're not a talker," I mumbled. "I would like to go into a frenzied rage, and I'm going to charge my new friend here and take three swings at them with my berserker axe." I picked up my d20 again. I rolled it, and rolled it, and rolled it again. "Twenty-eight, twenty-one, twenty-five," I announced. I picked three d12's from my dice bag and gave them a roll. "Fourteen, eleven, and eight slashing damage."

"Adrik is thrown back off his feet. Residual static still circulating and escaping from his now poofy and thick beard. Adrik then springs to life, angry and growling. He charges at the dragonborn as if nothing had happened. Axe held high above his head, Adrik swings with all his might. Each slash taking a chunk out of the dragonborn's natural scaled armor. Another swing slashing through the leathery stomach and spraying blood everywhere. And the final blow," Mr. R stopped to roll. "An uppercut swing slashes through the other two open wounds. The dragonborn lets out a loud roar."

"Yeah boy!" I shouted, pounding my chest.

"The dragonborn, in its anger, turns its head down at you." Mr. R squinted at me. "Now you die," he growled out. "And with that, the dragonborn takes the first scimitar and slashes at you—" Mr. R rolled. "Twenty-four hits. The first slash gashes across your chest, cutting through your thick beard and your muscular chest. The fighter spins with the momentum of the swing and goes to slash you with the other scimitar." He rolled again. "Twelve does not hit. For the final action to attack, the fighter goes to kick you square in the chest." He rolled one more time. "And a fifteen just hits. The kick sends you backward dealing a total of eighteen damage this round."

"Oh." I smiled. "We're just getting started! I hop back up and pull my bear fur off my shoulders, exposing my chest and the many tattoos that adorn my body. I use the flame symbol over my heart and cast Fire Bolt at the dragonborn."

"No freaking way," Rolen mumbled.

"Twenty-six to hit!" I cheered. "And they take thirteen fire damage."

Mr. R jotted something down before looking back up. "Adrik grazes his hand across the fire tattoo embedded in his chest. When his hand pulls away, the symbol no longer exists on his body, but a ball of flame illuminates his palm. He winds up and hurls the molten ball at the dragonborn. The flames swallow the fighter in a brief flash of light. Then, emerging from the smoldering sands, a slightly charred blue dragonborn hobbles closer to Adrik."

"And to finish my turn I'm going to charge them again and slash with my axe." I smiled. "Fourteen hit?"

Mr. R nodded.

"Then it's twelve slashing damage," I told him.

"As the fighter limps to its feet, Adrik rushes at it with an axe held high!" Mr. R narrated, "Bringing the axe down across the other three blackened and cauterized wounds. As the axe carves into the leathery skin, the wounds split open again. The dragonborn drops to a knee."

"Had enough yet?" I mocked.

Mr. R chuckled ominously and wiped the back of his hand against his chin. "I've had tougher than you for breakfast," the fighter snarled. "The dragonborn gets back to their feet, arms dangling at their side still holding the scimitars. In a weakened attempt to attack, the fighter flails their arms at you." Mr. R rolled. "Sixteen?"

"Hits," I answered.

"Dealing thirteen damage as the sword slices across your chest." Mr. R rolled again. "Swinging again. Eleven doesn't hit. The second swing comes just short of cutting you again. Making it your turn."

"Yield to the power of Frostbeard! From the kingdom under the mountain Yorr!" I roared. "And I lift my axe high over my head again and bring it down on their leg!" I rolled. "Fourteen?" I cringed.

"Just makes it," Mr. R smiled.

"I deal nine damage," I said. "And then I'm going to attack two more times with the axe." I rolled again. "Nineteen and twenty-three hit. I deal thirty-two damage total."

"After slamming your axe into the leg of the bloodied fighter before you, destroying their knee and dropping them to the ground. You swing up again, tearing into the many wounds across their chest, and finally bringing it down to their chest one last time," Mr. R described.

"How bad are they?" I asked.

"They're holding onto the last strands of life." He answered.

"Kneeling beside them I ask calmly, what brings you to this fight?"

"The crimes against my name. I am fighting to one day be

free and see my family once again." The dragonborn coughed out.

"Then you shall," I assured him. "I turn away from them and towards who I'm presuming is the king or leader." I shifted to Mr. R. "I will not kill Thray'dar! And Thray'dar shall not kill me."

"Then you both shall die—" The king began.

"Gimble! Now!" I shouted.

"I drop the Invisibility that I had cast last week before we stopped, grab Adrik, and cast Dimension Door into the king's box," Gimble explained.

"In all the commotion, Gimble appears in the ring beside Adrik, and then both are missing—" Mr. R narrated.

"I cast Dimension Door too. I move into the ring and grab Thray'dar," Lerissa interrupted.

"And Lerissa now appears in the ring momentarily before both she and Thray'dar vanish together," Mr. R continued.

"Rolen! Cloak! Now!" Lerissa instructed.

"I throw the cloak over them," Rolen said.

"Alright. You throw the cloak over Thray'dar and the five of you fade away into to the now panicked crowd," Mr. R began again. "Gimble and Adrik," he pointed at us. "You appear in a lavish room. Behind you is an opening to the pit where you stood moments ago. Before you there are multiple armed guards in full gear with spears pointed at you both. Behind them stands a human man. He's middle-aged, with dark black hair and a black goatee that are both peppered with streaks of grey hairs. An elegant crown atop his head."

Mr. R clicked the keyboard again and the image changed to a small but extravagant room as he'd described. Then six armed and armored guards appeared. Behind them hid the king. He wears very little, simply baggy white pants and a large, golden fabric belt wrapped around his lower abdomen.

"It's over, Charlemagne!" Gimble growled.

"Over?" Mr. R repeated in a low deep voice followed by his infamous evil chuckle. "How can it be over? You two are outnumbered, the whole city watched you brutally attack an innocent man, as well as their beloved king." He smiled a nasty smile. "I'm just waiting for your surrender."

"You know," Gimble laughed. "You're right. I drop to my knee." He bowed his head. "May I play a song for your highness?"

"I shall allow it if the dwarven filth kneels." The king spat.

"Kneel?" I scoffed. "Frostbeards don't kneel! Not to any crown but their own." I jammed my thumb into my chest.

"Then if you shall not do it willingly..." the king said through gritted teeth. He motions behind him and two guards move to Adrik, each grabbing an arm. While a third walks behind him, kicking at the back of his knees.

"You shouldn't have done that," I warned. "I'd like to throw the two holding my arms into each other before slamming Ralph Macchio back there into the pit."

"Give me a strength check," Mr. R pointed his pencil at me.

"Eighteen," I answered.

"With grace, you slam the two nearest you into each other You then turn. A small bit of steam escapes your nose as you rush the guard behind you who had kicked at the back of your knees! And with a Wilhelm scream, the guard plummets into the sandy ring below," Mr. R narrated.

Gimble let out a heavy sigh. "I cast Dispel Magic while he does that."

"Who or what do you target?" Mr. R asked.

"The king's crown." He smiled, and then to the tune of Britney Spears' *Oops I Did It Again*, Jake sang out, "Oops I screwed up your plan. Gonna see you again. Ooo baby, baby. Oops, I screwed up your spell."

"As Adrik finishes off his collection of guards, Gimble pulls out the violin and plays his tune to dispel magic," Mr. R continued. He let out another ominous chuckle. "You think a little song will distract me, Gnome? You worthless halfling—" The king scoffed. "What is happening? What have you done to me?" He panicked. Looking at his arms and feeling his torso. "You both watch as the king's form begins to fade in and out. Like a TV with bad reception, until in the human king's space, stands a kobold in a crown and baggy white pants."

"Grab him, Adrik!" Gimble shouted.

"I charge the kobold!" I smiled.

"Still in his bull-like rage, Adrik turns and begins rushing the kobold, whose first instinct now is to run," Mr. R said.

"I chase him." I growled. "I love a good chase."

"What's your speed?" Mr. R asked.

"Thirty-five." I answered him. "Seventy if we're running."

"As the kobold turns towards the door and books it. Adrik pursues him, pushing past the other three guards who now stand dazed in the room as if they had been stunned," Mr. R began.

"I follow behind!" Gimble added.

"You both now go running through hallways, down a set of stairs, and across a courtyard before you end up outside in the streets of the underground market. Roll me a perception check."

"Ten," I blurted out.

"Twenty-two," Jacob chuckled.

"Gimble, you notice people jumping and scurrying out of the way. Between the masses of legs at your height, you see a kobold, shoving his way through the dense crowd," Mr. R continued.

"Follow me," Gimble instructed me.

"You both set off into the tightly packed crowd. Pushing and shoving your way through—"

"I split from following Gimble and move to flank him," I interrupted.

"In your pursuit, just as he seems to be getting away. Adrik comes from out of nowhere and tackles the kobold into a roll," Mr. R described.

"I would like to keep him pinned under my knee," I told him.

"I catch up with Adrik and then cast Message to Lerissa."

THE SHADESTONE UNDERGROUND

"Lerissa, Rolen, Torinn, Ront. After receiving Thray'dar and scurrying out of the arena, you are thrown into the hustle and bustle of the market area. Beings of all shapes, sizes, professions, and dress move in every direction," Mr. R narrated.

"Hoods up," Ront instructed them.

Each of them mimed putting up their hoods.

"Lerissa, in your head, you begin hearing Gimble's voice echo." Mr. R pointed to Gimble.

"Lerissa, can you hear me?" Gimble asked.

"Yes. I hear you," Lerissa answered. "Where are you two?"

"Outside," Gimble told her. "We caught Charlemagne. Where are you guys?"

"Outside," Lerissa answered. "Can I roll to percept for them?" she asked Mr. R.

He nodded.

Lerissa shook her head. "Well, I know a seven isn't going to find them."

"Where are we in relation to the arena?" Gimble asked.

"You two are both against the outer wall of the arena. Maybe a couple hundred meters from where you exited," Mr. R explained.

"I cast Message again. We're against the arena's outer wall. Not too far from the king's entrance," Gimble said, his hand to his ear.

"Do I know where that is?" Laura asked.

Mr. R pursed his lips and clicked his tongue for a moment. "Yeah." He nodded. "I'd say you're aware of it. It's up and around the corner from where you're at."

"Don't move. We're heading to you," Lerissa said to Gimble.

"You five make your way to the other two. Pushing your way through the crowds of people going this way and that way. But when you finally see them, you see Adrik kneeling over a helpless kobold still fighting trying to get free. A crown still fitted on his head," Mr. R described.

"This is him?" Ront asked.

"This is him." Gimble nodded. "I dispelled his crown. It was the arcane focus that was keeping the guards under his control and keeping him disguised."

"How did you know?" Rolen asked.

"What city has a king?" Gimble raised his eyebrow. "Especially one so lawless and sketchy as Shadestone."

"I guess that makes sense." Rolen shrugged.

"Then what do we do with this slimy filth?" Torinn snarled.

"Well," Ront spoke up. "I would like to get a drink if you're all willing?" He leaned in towards Mr. R. "And I know an amazing little place a couple blocks from here where you and I can get a little privacy to discuss... business."

"Charlemagne spits at you," Mr. R rolled. "And he gets you right in the eye."

Ront chuckled as he wiped away the imaginary spit. "We're going to have a lot of fun talking! I think we might even become great friends."

"I pick him up and tie his hands," I said.

"Let's go," Ront grumbled. "And I kick the little lizard scum in front of me."

"You eight begin walking through the busy streets. Taking a left here, a right there, and so on until you reach a familiar tavern." Mr. R clicked his keyboard and the screen in the table showed an image of a massive corner tavern. The sign hanging there read *One-eyed Smugglers Inn and Tavern*.

The hotel-sized tavern went on for seven or eight floors. Mr. R took a paper from behind his screen and placed it in front of us.

One-eyed Smuggler's Inn and Tavern

Rooms
1 bed

10gp

2 bed

25gp

Private room

35gp

Special private room

50-100gp (Price may vary on beings' size)

Room service

15gp

Clean up services

15-100gp
(prices vary by blood and body count)

***meals served all day!
Tavern opened to all patrons
Limit six prisoners per party**

"I waltz my way in, dragging our new friend behind me by his restraints." Ront smiled. "I go up to the check-in desk and knock on the counter."

"From under the desk. A grumpy, old, and grey goblin traipses up the step stool and stands behind the desk." Mr. R clicked the keyboard again.

An image of a nasty looking goblin in a suit appeared behind a counter. His left eye was blinded with a scar across it. The scar ran from his hairline, or lack thereof, and stopped at a hole in his cheek that exposed some of the teeth hidden in his mouth.

"Welcome to the One-eyed Smugglers Inn," Mr. R said, his voice gravelly and scratchy like someone who smoked way too long and then screamed for years. "What can I help ya with?"

"I need a *special* private room, my good sir. And I slide the goblin seventy-five gold pieces." Ront grinned.

"One special private room for ya and—" he squinted at the group. "I'm sorry sir, only six prisoners per party. I coun' seven 'ere," the goblin grumbled.

"Oh no, no, no." Ront shook his head. "I've only got one prisoner. I drag Charlemagne off his feet and up over the counter. This is who I'd like to take into that special room. These here are my companions." He gestured around to us all.

"Companions?" The goblin scratched his chin. "And ya slave, correct?" he asked, pointing at Lerissa.

Lerissa's eyes flared. "Excuse me—"

"I'm sorry, my good sir," Ront threw a hand up to stop her. "This is my good friend and companion. She will be aiding me in my conversation with my little prisoner friend here. As well as my bardic companion over here." He gestures to Gimble.

"M-my apologies," the goblin bowed his head. "I 'ave never met a free tieflin' before." He bowed his head. "One special private room. Deluxe sized fo' my incompetence. Please enjoy." Mr. R reached under the table. "He pulls out a key from under the counter and hands it to you." Mr. R reached across to Lerissa and pretended to hand her a key.

She scowled at him.

"Thank you, my good sir." Ront accepted the key. "Let's go, cretin. I drag Charlemagne off the counter and to the room."

"Rolen," Lerissa turned to her brother. "Will you take Thray'dar, Adrik, and Tor, find a table and heal up. Especially those two." She pointed at Mr. R and me. "They're going to need it after that battle."

Rolen nodded.

"Let's go figure out what the pipsqueak knows!" Ront smiled.

"Alright, before we do that," Mr. R said. "Rolen, Adrik, and Torinn, you walk deeper into the lobby area of the tavern. It's much larger than the type of tavern you guys normally visit. The ceiling runs all the way to the top of the eighth floor, with an open courtyard kind of feel. You could count each floor as they cascade further towards the top. The four of you weave through tables and chairs until you find an empty table large enough for your party. You four sit down. Weapons placed beside you or on the table. What do you do?"

"I take Adrik and cast Cure Wounds. Healing him for nineteen hit points." Ben explained.

"I do the same for Thray'dar," Torinn said. "I'm going to cast mine at the fifth level since they're in much worse condition." he rolled his dice. "Healing them for twenty-nine. Not much more. But it's something."

"They breathe in before speaking up." Mr. R drew a similar breath. "Thank you." His voice went deep and grumbled in my chest and ears. "Thank you all for your mercy," He looked at me. "And for helping me escape that hell hole."

"Don't sweat it." Rolen shrugged. "We know the terrible crap that these nasty people have been doing to the world. We've been tracking them down in search of their leader. He disappeared from our grasp a while back. And took some people important to us."

"You mean Charlemagne is a pawn?" Thray'dar asked, puzzled.

"Well yeah. He and many others are just pawns. They're a part of a greater group called Death's Empire. Formerly Death's Hand." Rolen explained. "A cult once dedicated to necromancy in service to the Raven Queen, now a genocidal empire attempting to rid the world of those who oppose them. Wiping out entire clans and kingdoms. And their leader is a necromancer named Greg." He took a drink.

"We've been tracking down his high-powered followers and soldiers. Many of whom are hiding in plain sight. Much like Charlemagne's crown, they have items of arcane focus that control and confuse the people living in the areas that they force their way into," Torinn continued.

"Rolen, will you give me a perception check?" Mr. R asked.

He rolled. "Eighteen."

"As you and Torinn are explaining this to Thray'dar, a couple of figures begin to catch your eye. In the adjacent corner, a hooded humanoid being leans back in their chair, boots up on the table. Their glowing eyes peer through the darkness of the hood, watching you," Mr. R depicted. "At another table, two goliaths and a halfling keep glancing over at you. And finally, an elven man stands from his table at the far end of the room, and begins slowly making his way towards you all."

"Don't be alarmed," Rolen said. "But they found us. We're surrounded by them. This whole room."

"H-how do you know?" Thray'dar mumbled.

"They're not subtle. The elf over there slowly moving in on us." Rolen pointed randomly. "He's the lead. He's going to come sit with us trying to distract us while those big ones over there," He pointed over his shoulder. "They're going to start getting up—"

"They get up from their table as you say that," Mr. R said.

"And move over to the exit, cutting off our escape. Then the hooded figure with his feet up over there," Rolen pointed randomly again. "Will get up and look for the rest of our group."

"How did they find us here?" Thray'dar asked.

"The goblin from the front." Torinn joined in.

"He sold us out," Rolen finished. "Lerissa gave us up. When they made comment on her being a slave. It's their give-away. They believe that tieflings are inferior and should be slaves. When she went off the handle at the comment, he knew who we were. A normal group would have blown past it."

"They think we fell into their trap," I whispered. "But really, we have them trapped."

"Before that," Mr. R interrupted. "Let's go to Ront, Lerissa, and Gimble. You three enter a chamber and close the thick wooden door behind you. To your right sits a counter with all types of chairs. Under the counter, cords and cords of wood fill the space. The only light source is the dim beam of sunlight that seeps in through the two small windows opposite the door. The grey, stone, abysmal room gives off the perfect interrogation vibe."

"I would like our new friend to have a seat." Ront smiled. "But I make him a little leash so he doesn't get any funny ideas."

"And I cast Arcane Lock on the door," Lerissa added.

"As Ront ties down the squirming kobold into the beaten wooden chair, Lerissa speaks an incantation and the door glistens with an arcane energy," Mr. R described.

"Perfect." Ront chuckled. "Now, shall we begin? First, is there a fireplace in this room?"

"There is on the wall behind Charlemagne," Mr. R answered.

"Gimble, will you light that fire for me?" Ront asked.

"Sure." Gimble nodded. "I move to the fireplace and start a nice fire with my tinderbox."

"Fwoosh!" Mr. R roared. "The fire sparks to life."

"Now, Charlemagne, I have some questions for you," Ront said. Rolling his d4 between his palms. "I move over to the fireplace and set one of my normal daggers into the flames. Then I circle back behind Charlemagne." He sipped his soda. "Where is he?"

"I don't know who you're talking about," the kobold hissed. "And if I did, why would I tell a disgusting creature like you?" Mr. R pretended to spit on the floor. "Filthy half-being. Both you and the half-elf. Makes me sick!"

"Well that's such a bummer." Ront shrugged. "I thought could have been such great pals." He cracked his knuckles. "Oh well. I take out the Raven dagger and press it against his back."

"You press the tip of the blade into the kobold's back and watch as he straightens up," Mr. R narrated.

"What?" Charlemagne growled. "Are you gonna kill me because I don't like inferior beings?"

"I'd like to slowly dig the tip into his back," Ront said.

"You watch Charlemagne crane his neck as he fights the urge to show any pain," Mr. R described.

"Now I warn you," Ront whispered as he leaned across the table. "This dagger has a bit of a bite to it, especially when you lie. So I'm going to ask one more time. Where is Greg?"

"I already told you," Charlemagne hissed. "I don't know who you're talking about!"

"Before I harm him further, does he have the mark of the empire on him?" Ront asked.

"Give me a perception check," Mr. R answered.

Liam rolled, "Twenty-three."

"On the back of his neck to under his jaw, there is a thick scar in the shape of a raven surrounded by the letter D." Mr. R depicted.

"Then I set my hand out like a doctor in surgery," Ront smiled.

"I move to hand him the dagger from the fire," Gimble added.

"It's a shame really," Ront sighed. "I was hoping you wouldn't upset my master by lying. But hey, this will hurt you a lot more than it will hurt me. And I switch blades. Putting the red-hot blade into the same wound."

"You hear the fizzle of blood evaporating against the hot metal and the smell of cooked alligator fills the air as Charlemagne lets out a cry of pain," Mr. R described.

"Now tell me again." Ront twisted his hand. Indicating further digging with the dagger. "Where is he?"

"Tr'heymount!" Charlemagne let out in a wail of pain. "He was in Tr'heymount last I spoke to him!" He was panting for air. "He's going to kill me! He's going to slaughter us!"

"Maybe you," Ront shrugged. "But for now, you should fear us." He gestured to Lerissa. "I believe it's your turn."

"Thank you." She nodded. "I squat down in front of Charlemagne and place my hand on his knee." She gave a warm smile.

It was that Laura smile that lit up the room. I always felt safe and warm in that smile. A smile I recognized the feel of—pressed against my cheek—pressed against my lips!

"Where is Greg hiding the others?" Lerissa broke through my daydream. "Where did he hide the other wizard girl? The little gnome child? The human man?"

"They—I can't!" He fought. "I'm already dead! Any more and he will kill my whole species!"

"Another shame." Lerissa frowned. "I cast Shocking Grasp." She rolled. "Twenty-two to hit." She rolled again. "Fifteen lightning damage."

"As you shake your head in pity at the sad kobold, a current of electricity begins to circle around your arm before discharging into Charlemagne's leg," Mr. R said before scanning his notes. "He lets out a grunt before his snout slams shut. His eyes rolling back into his skull. When the spell finishes, seconds later, all the electricity leaves his muscles. Charlemagne slumps over, limp in the chair."

"Shit!" Ront cried out. "We needed him, Riss!"

"I-I-I—" She stammered. "I didn't think it would kill him! It was a cantrip. They don't kill anything."

"You're level sixteen," Ront reminded her. "Your cantrips are powerful when it comes to low-level lizard freaks."

Lerissa crossed her eyes, annoyed. "I guess you're right." She rolled her lips in and crinkled her nose. "What should we do then?"

"We should get out of here before they start attacking the guys in the lobby—"

Mr. R interrupted by slamming his fist on the table four times. "Open up! We know you're in there!" A heavy voice rumbled. "Don't make this any harder than it needs to be!"

"Well, crap. Looks like we're fighting our way out of another tavern." Gimble laughed. "Get behind the door. When I say, Lerissa drop the Lock spell," he instructed. "I turn Charlemagne in the chair around and set it facing the door."

"The being from behind the door seems to be slamming against the door trying to break it down," Mr. R said.

"Lerissa. Drop it!" Gimble smiled.

"The arcane shimmer of the door dissipates and a hulking behemoth slams through," Mr. R narrated.

"I'd like to cast Sleep on the three intruders," Gimble said. He leaned back in his chair with his arms behind his head. "Hush little monster doesn't say a word, Gimble's gonna give you a world of hurt," he sang out.

"After barging into the room and hearing the somber tune from the bard, the two hulking goliaths crash to the floor in an instant slumber. Behind them in the doorway, a mangled looking halfling is asleep against the doorframe." Mr. R shook his head, smiling.

"Nice work," Ront whispered. He shot two thumbs up at Gimble. "I carefully move around the sleeping nitwits and their babysitter, and book it to the lobby."

"I follow," Gimble and Lerissa said together.

"The three of you make your way back towards the tavern lobby. Rolen, Adrik, and Torinn, you're approached by the elven man. His pale skin contrasts with the dark leathers and cloak he wears. A bright pink scar adorns his eye, causing the deep purple irises to pop. He takes a seat at your table." Mr. R sipped his drink. "You folks are not from around here," His voice calm and still, the kind of voice that chills you to the bone.

"And what gives you that idea?" I retorted.

Mr. R eyed Torinn for a moment. "Two dragonborns out in the open in Shadestone. That's two more than this town usually has. And not to mention the tiefling, half-orc, and half-elf not being in chains and rags."

Rolen's face began to scrunch with anger.

"Well maybe we're just not as closed-minded," I shot back. "That tiefling happens to be one of the strongest wizards to ever live."

"Oh, I'm well aware." A smile grew across Mr. R's face. "Now if you four don't mind coming with me, quietly and calmly."

"Well then." I chuckled. "You don't know who you're dealing with." I cracked my neck by turning my head from side to side. "I flip the table on him." I rolled my d20. "Seventeen!"

"With a grin across his face, Adrik erupts from his chair, sending the table flying on top of the elf." Mr. R rolled. "The elf man manages to move out from under the table in a blur. The table comes crashing to the ground as Ront bursts into the lobby, followed by Lerissa and Gimble."

"I guess we made it just in time." Lerissa sighed.

Mr. R chuckled. "Everyone roll me initiative."

TRASHING THE TAVERN

"Sixteen!" Jacob called out.

"Six," I groaned.

"Ten," Liam frowned.

"Five," Ben sighed.

"Fifteen," Laura said.

"Well crap," Daryl cursed. "Natural One."

Everyone looked at Daryl in disbelief.

"I guess I picked the wrong set for that one," he shrugged.

"Alright," Mr. R said as he looked up from writing. "As the table is thrown and the elf man jumps out of the way, he throws three daggers at Adrik, Torinn, and Rolen." He rolled three times. "Twenty-two on Adrik. Seven on Torinn. Eleven on Rolen."

"Hits," I sighed.

"Miss," Daryl smiled.

"My armor class is eleven. Does that mean it hits?" Ben asked.

"If it meets, it hits," Mr. R explained. "So Adrik and Rolen, you both take four damage as the daggers find their marks in your chests. Not deep enough to cause major damage. But they cut pretty well into your muscle tissue."

"You're gonna regret that," I growled.

"Gimble, you're up," Mr. R said, pointing his pencil.

"Is the elf rogue guy within thirty feet of me?" Jake asked.

"No," Mr. R answered. He fiddled around with his laptop and didn't look up for a few minutes.

Mr. R dragged a window onto the screen. It was a map of the room. And it was huge. He reached back and grabbed the miniatures off the shelf behind him. He placed Gimble, Lerissa, and Ront together on the far side of the map. He turned back to grab the last three minis and placed them together across the map in front of me. He wheeled out from behind the table and over to another shelf of miniatures in the room. It looked like a china cabinet full of statues of all sizes. He looked around for a second before reaching far back on one of the shelves. He pulled out a blue dragonborn piece, a hooded figure, and an elven mini in dark gear.

Mr. R moved back to his spot at the table and placed the other three minis on the map. He positioned the blue drag-onborn and the elf with the cluster in front of me, and the other hooded figure in the middle of the map.

"It would take all your movement but then he would be within thirty feet," Mr. R continued.

"Then I will do that. I'm going to..." Jake leaned over the table and moved his mini. "Five, ten, fifteen, twenty, twenty-five," he counted, moving his mini through the squares. "I land here and cast Hold Person on the elf, man, thing, guy."

"Wisdom save?" Mr. R asked.

Jacob nodded.

Mr. R rolled. "What is your spell DC?"

"Seventeen," Jacob said.

"He fails." Mr. R scrunched his face. "What happens to him?"

"As I run up singing *Stop in the Name of Love* by The Supremes, the rogue freezes in place. He's paralyzed, unable to do anything until he succeeds on a wisdom save or the spell wears off in a minute," Jacob narrated.

"Alright, Lerissa." Mr. R pointed at Laura with his pencil again.

She swished her cheeks back and forth, back and forth. Scanning through her binder, she pulled out her player's manual and flipped through the spells in the back. "Okay!" she blurted out. "I'm going to move over behind the hooded man and cast Charm Person on him."

Mr. R rolled and then rolled a second time. "What's your spell DC?"

"Eighteen," Laura reminded him.

"Fails the wisdom save," Mr. R said.

"Alright," Lerissa folded her arms. "Now as a wizard of the school of enchantment, I can erase the memory of events when a target is charmed. So I would like to erase the memory of when they were given the mission to find us."

"For that, I will need you to roll me a spell attack," Mr. R asked.

She rolled. "Twenty-one."

"As far as you're aware, the hooded figure has no hostilities or charges against you anymore." Mr. R wrote something down. "Ront, your move." He pointed to his nephew.

"Let's dance!" Ront smiled. "I pull out the Raven dagger

and one of my poison daggers." He squinted at Mr. R. "I throw the raven dagger at the wall behind the rogue, teleport, and then that should give me sneak attack when I stab him in the back with my other dagger."

"I need a dexterity check first. If he succeeds then you can attack," Mr. R explained.

Liam rolled. "Fifteen on the dex check."

"Now roll your attack," Mr. R nodded.

"Twenty-two hits." Liam scooped up a handful of d6's and then plopped a d4 into the pile. He shook the collection between both his hands and dropped them on the table. He pulled all the dice together and calculated. "Six, nine, eighteen, twenty-eight, forty-one on sneak attack damage, three piercing damage, six after modifiers. And last, four, eight, eleven poison damage. That totals to fifty-eight damage!" He let out a big sigh. "Too much math! It's the weekend. Why am I doing math?"

"Ront, you throw your raven dagger at the wall behind the frozen rogue," Mr. R began. "And in a puff of black smoke, you bamf behind the man. You take your poison dagger and drive it deep into the rogue's back. You hear an internal whine of pain as the poison from your blade sets into the wound. Unable to move, you watch as his neck muscles begin to tense even tighter than before." Mr. R rolled a few dice. "And as you pull the blade from the wound, the veins around his wound began to bulge bright purple against the pale skin. That ends your turn. Moving on." He rolled again behind the screen. "The hooded man in front of Lerissa rises to his feet." He grabbed the figure on the table and held it. "And he walks from the room. Unsure about why he is where he's at. Making it Adrik's turn."

"Yar!" I cheered. "I'd like to move against the dying elf,

man, person, thing. And I want to lift him up and slam him into a table."

"Give me a strength check." Mr. R nodded.

I rolled. "Non-natural twenty."

"Like watching a WWE match, you all witness as Adrik, the dwarven barbarian, lifts the paralyzed elf high over his head. And with showmanship and grace, falls backward, slamming the elf through a wooden table!" Mr. R narrated. "A faint grunt comes from the elf on the floor." He scanned his notes. "Rolen, your turn."

"I move to the painfully paralyzed elf man," Rolen began. "I cast Produce Flames and cauterize the stab wound in his back." He rolled. "I assume I have to hit, so twenty-five. I seal the wound but also cause fifteen fire damage in the process."

"With a flick of your wrist, a small flame is produced in your palm. You move it towards the now black wound. The scent of burning skin fills the room and muted screams of pain come from the elf." Mr. R narrated. "As you finish the incantation and seal his wound, his veins begin to bulge under his skin. Dark and black."

"Do I know what is happening?" Ben asked.

"Give me a nature check," Mr. R said.

"Twenty-seven," Ben answered.

"You recognize this as the spread of serpent venom," Mr. R explained. "The venom spreads through the veins. The venom coagulating with the blood until it's almost sludge, blocking the veins and restricting the flow of blood to the brain. The victim will succumb to a heart attack and die within minutes."

Rolen's eyes grew wide as he drew in a deep breath. "Can I cast Protect From Poison?"

"You don't have another action do you?" Mr. R asked.

Ben shook his head.

"Then no. Not until your next turn," Mr. R explained.

"Then I end my turn." Ben frowned.

"Torinn, your turn." Mr. R pointed his pencil.

"I move to Rolen and the rogue and cast Protect From Poison on the elf," Torinn said.

"Torinn, you bend down to your knees and place your hand on the dying elf's chest. As your amulet begins to glow, you notice the black veins in his neck are beginning to fade away," Mr. R narrated. "The little bit of color returning to his face and his chest returns to its normal up and down motion."

"Don't make me regret letting him live," Torinn warned Rolen.

"As the elf returns to the land of the living." Mr. R rolled. "You feel a piercing pain in your side. You move to look and see a dagger now protruding from it!"

Rolen's lips pursed before he shouted, "Mother—"

"Roll me a constitution saving throw!" Mr. R cut him off.

"Nine," Rolen rolled his lips with anger.

"As you move to try and react to the hole in your side, drenching your clothes in blood, your muscles begin to seize up." Mr. R continued.

"What happened to my Hold Person spell?" Gimble argued.

Without saying a word, Mr. R held up a large blue d20, and it was a natural twenty.

"Well, I'll be a monkey's uncle!" Jacob laughed.

"Well stop being an uncle and help me." Rolen growled through his teeth.

"It's my turn, right?" Jacob asked.

Mr. R nodded.

"I cast Hold Person again on this bum!" Gimble shouted.

Mr. R rolled. "He does not succeed. The elf tries to get back up and escape from you. He stops motionless mid-step, frozen in place by the incantation cast again by Gimble."

Mr. R pointed his pencil over to Laura.

"I cast Geas on the rogue," Lerissa announced. "And command him to cease his attack on us."

Mr. R nodded and rolled some more. "What's your spell DC?"

"Eighteen," Laura reminded him.

"Yeah, no." Mr. R chuckled. "He doesn't save." He scribbled in his notes. "Although paralyzed in place, the elven rogue now is compelled not to attack any of you."

"We need to go!" Lerissa blurted out.

"Ront," Mr. R said turning to his nephew.

"I grab Thray'dar and head—is there a back door?" Ront asked.

"Give me a perception check," Mr. R answered.

Liam rolled. "Twenty-three."

"There is a second door in the back of the lobby area," Mr. R explained.

"Then that's where we go," Ront finished.

"Okay." Mr. R rolled a few times behind his screen before looking up at me. "Adrik."

"I move to grab Rolen and follow behind Ront," I said.

"Are you carrying him?" Mr. R raised his eyebrow. "Or helping him to the doorway?"

"Is he still paralyzed?" I asked.

Mr. R nodded.

"Then I pick him up."

"Roll a strength check."

"Eighteen."

"You charge towards the paralyzed Rolen sitting on the ground," Mr. R began. "In a swift motion you bend down and throw him over your shoulder before turning towards the exit." He turned his attention to Rolen. "Roll me a wisdom-saving throw."

"Eighteen," Ben answered.

"As Adrik barrels towards you and throws his arm into your stomach, hoisting you up on his shoulder. You feel the paralysis fade like melting ice," Mr. R described.

"Put me down!" Rolen shouted at me.

"Too late!" I shouted back.

Rolen rolled his eyes and folded his arms, sinking into his chair.

Mr. R turned to Torinn and pointed his eraser at him.

"I follow behind Ront and Adrik." Torinn shrugged.

"Turning on your heels, you race out the back door," Mr. R narrated. He shuffled through some papers and rolled some dice before looking back up and pointing at Gimble. "Your move."

"L-l-let's get out of here, Scoob," Gimble stuttered in his best Shaggy voice, nudging Lerissa.

"Right, Raggy!" Lerissa laughed as she mimicked Scooby-Doo.

"Do you both follow your group?" Mr. R asked.

They looked at each other and nodded.

"As the last two climb through the back door, you all find yourselves crammed in a tight alleyway," Mr. R explained. "Ront, you are unable to move freely and having to sidestep to move anywhere. While Gimble, you can move up and down this alleyway with ease."

"I'm pretty wedged in here, right?" Liam asked.

Mr. R eyed him for a moment before nodding to confirm.

"Awesome," Liam grinned. And it was like looking at a younger looking Mr. R. Same devious grin. "I would like to press myself between the walls and climb my way to the rooftops."

Mr. R blinked for a moment. "Give me—" he flipped through his notes and binders for a moment. "Give me an acrobatics check."

Ront rolled and the cringe on his face gave it all away. "Ten." He sighed.

"Could have been worse," Daryl tried to assure him.

Mr. R rolled and scrunched his face in thought. "Welp," he popped his lips. "You manage to fit your body just right between the walls. It's a slow process, but you manage to make your way to the rooftops."

"Wonderful," Liam smiled. "Can I percept for any clues of a safe haven?" he leaned closer. "Maybe somewhere marked with Thieves' Cant?"

Mr. R's eyes grew wide. He fought between smiling and frowning as he thought about his answer, a very confusing display of emotion on his face. "Give me a perception check," he asked as he rifled through more papers.

"Non-natural twenty." Liam leaned back in his chair.

Mr. R frantically tore through his binders. "Okay," he nodded. "Give me one sec."

It was rare that we ever caught Mr. R off guard, but he showed no sign that he was panicked.

"There we are," he said as he thumbed through a stack of papers he'd pulled from his binders. "You peer out into the vast city. Buildings that almost kiss the cavern's ceiling." Mr. R fiddled with his laptop a bit before throwing up an image of the Shadestone underground.

It resembled a massive middle eastern cityscape. One you might see in an Indiana Jones movie. But this city wasn't in the midst of an endless, sun-beaten, sandy desert. It was deep inside a colossal cave. Beams of light poured in through the many entrance holes in the cave walls. It was truly from the masterful mind of Mr. R and his imagination.

"As you scan the horizon, listening to faint conversations about the buying and trading of illegal items and substances, you pick up on a language that you have not heard in ages." Mr. R cleared his throat. "Sehya bouroro, mour'toowa sentaya, m'hash lampura krata."

Mr. R passed a piece of paper to Liam. He unfolded it and read.

"Good to know." Liam nodded. "Now where is it at?"

"Where is what?" Jacob asked.

"Nothing," Liam said. "Not yet at least."

"Can I join him up top?" Jacob asked.

"How would you like to get up there?" Mr. R questioned.

"The easy way," Jacob chuckled. "With magic. I want to Dimension Door up to him."

"With a blink, Gimble bamfs from the middle of the tight alleyway and appears on the rooftops behind Ront," Mr. R narrated.

"Where is what?" Gimble repeated himself.

Ront sighed. "I'm looking for a safe haven for us," he explained. "There are hidden symbols all around the world. And only those trained in the skills of rogues like myself are able to decipher them." He sat up in his chair, holding a posture of high importance.

"Well I'll be." Gimble laughed. He leaned his elbow on the table and motioned Ront closer. "I'm looking into taking some lessons in being a rogue. Mind giving me some pointers?"

Ront's stance dropped. That feeling of being better than everyone else was diminished. Like watching a drunk person sober up at the realization of something they did.

"Y-yeah, sure." Ront blinked. "Um," he hummed. He was stalling while he processed what just happened. "Did I find anything that stuck out to me?" he asked, diverting his gaze to his uncle.

"Before you were given company, you saw a set of flags across the way. A red flag over and under a green triangle flag," Mr. R explained. "Indicating a thieves' guild of some sort."

"I point out across the horizon at the flags," Ront began. "What do those flags mean?"

Gimble looked at Mr. R, who nodded in a silent response.

"There's a thieves' guild over there. A place for folks like us." Gimble smiled.

Ront's face shifted into a shocked expression. "How did you know that?" he asked.

"Well, wasn't it obvious?" Gimble shrugged. "Anyone who has trained or learned the ways of a rogue would be able to understand a visual sign with Thieves' Cant."

"Did I miss something?" Liam questioned, scanning everyone's face.

We all shrugged with the same confused expression he had.

"I leveled up." Jacob laughed. "I took a level in rogue. Figured I could try to become a little more useful."

"That's great," Lerissa interjected. "But if you both don't mind putting the rulers away, we're still running for our lives!"

"Right." Ront snapped his fingers. "Out across the way is a thieves' guild. Maybe we could find safe-haven there."

"How do we get there?" Lerissa asked.

"Can you all make it up here?" Ront suggested.

"Well," Lerissa said, scrunching her nose in thought. "I can Dimension Door me and one other." She broke off and searched her handbook. "But I don't have much in being able to move everyone."

Liam chewed the inside of his cheeks. "Can I figure out where it's at from below?" He asked Mr. R.

"Give me an intelligence check," Mr. R answered.

Ront shook his head as he looked at his roll. "Nine?"

"You can't seem to place together exactly how far it is or how many blocks it would take," Mr. R explained.

"Well crap," Ront muttered. "How should we get there then? I can't lose sight of these flags or we will lose our way."

"Why don't you guide us from up there?" Torinn spoke up. "Stay close to the edge of the buildings so we can see you. From there we can find it."

"I guess that could work," Gimble shrugged.

"I don't mean to be a Debbie-downer," Rolen interrupted. "But I kind of have a hole in my side that is bleeding out. If we could kind of hurry before they find us and widen that hole?"

"Get goin'!" I said.

"Alright." Ront nodded. "I start making my way to the marked building."

SCUM & VILLAINY

"Bobbing and weaving through the city, and shoving through tight alleys, large crowds, and even a herd of goats and pigs, you all manage to find the marked building," Mr. R narrated. "It's an abysmal looking place on the wrong end of the city. The front windows are dark and hard to see through. The front door is a large iron door, and the flow of foot traffic in and out is heavy."

"I come down from the rooftops and join everyone," Ront said.

"I follow him," Gimble added.

"I go into the door," Ront directed. "Follow me and stay close, okay?" He was staring at me now.

"Yeah, yeah." I waved him off. "I can handle my own," I assured him.

"That's what I'm afraid of," Ront sighed.

"As you swing the iron door open, you're met with a full tavern of beings of all sizes, colors, smells. There are beaten and bloody beings. There are pampered and lavish beings. Elves sitting with dwarves and orcs sitting with goblins. So many different beings, and all of them dressed in the same black armor and hood that Ront wears," Mr. R narrated.

"I lead the group to a dark corner in the back," Ront said. "As far away from everyone as I can."

"There's an open table in the back of the bar," Mr. R depicted.

"I take it," Ront blurted. "You all sit here. Do not talk to anyone. Do not look at anyone. Don't even breathe on anyone. Every single being in here is dangerous. You could lose both your life and your gold in the same second. Just stay put, let me do some asking around. I'm going to try to get us out of Shadestone and off to Tr'heymount as fast and safely as possible."

"Alright." Mr. R nodded. "You all take a seat at the empty table in the far back end of the tavern. Between the brightly colored gear you all wear, to the even brighter colors of your two dragonborn companions, you can feel the eyes following you."

"I would like to opt out of sitting, and go with Ront," Gimble spoke up.

"No!" Ront jumped. "No! This is not the place for a beginner. They will kill you before you can even get the first syllable out."

"But you're working diplomacy, my friend." Gimble smiled. "And who doesn't need a bard to help with that?"

Ront pursed his lips together so tight, I thought his teeth were going to tear through them.

"Fine," Ront huffed. "But unless things are going astray, I do the talking and the work! Give me your arm."

Gimble eyed him for a moment before setting his arm out on the table.

"I take his arm and carve the symbol for Draven's Guild," Ront said. He stood from his chair with a sharpie in hand, grabbed Gimble's arm and drew the letter D or it might have been a sideways triangle. Then he drew two diagonal lines off the back. It looked like a fish whose tail fin didn't connect. Or if a D had a backward K attached to their vertical sides.

"Gimble you take one point of damage as Ront carves this symbol into your arm," Mr. R began. "It hurts for a while and is a bit of a mess—"

"I take out some cloth, tear off a swath of it, and dip it in a glass of whiskey before tying it with another dry piece to heal and try to keep it clean," Gimble interrupted. "I also down the rest of that whiskey in an attempt to dull that pain."

"Wow, I made him drink!" Ront laughed. "Am I that bad to be with?"

"Well when you're not expecting to be carved up like a turkey, you gotta make do," Gimble said, shaking his head. "Let's do this!"

"I guess we're going." Ront shrugged. "Don't move!" He pointed at me.

I threw my hands up in defense. "I never cause the trouble. It just seems to find me."

"Don't do it!" Ront squinted.

"So," Mr. R cut back in, "You two go and search the place?"

Ront and Gimble nodded.

"What are you looking for, specifically?" Mr. R asked.

"Draven," Ront said.

"Alright." Mr. R shrugged. He began rifling through more papers. "Roll me a perception check."

Liam rolled. "Sixteen?"

"You wander around for a little bit. Listening here and there, trying to get a lead on where Draven is at," Mr. R narrated. "There's a lot of talk about the last score someone took or the hit they just completed. But one conversation catches your ear." He cleared his throat. "Yeah, I went ou' with the boss! Took me an' me boys to Sumarna fo' a lil' bit o' pilla-gin'. Los' me eye to a beautiful elven girl! She was feisty! Made it all the more fun—"

"I dash at the boasting buffoon and pin him by his throat with my dagger nicely pressed against his Adam's apple," Ront interrupted.

"What in the blazes—" Mr. R choked out before Ront cut him off again.

"I don't quite like your story there my friend." He grimaced. "Ya know the whole war crimes bit. Forcing yourself on an innocent woman. Not okay, my friend. Not okay."

"Yeah?" The man chuckled. "And wha' you gonna do 'bout it?"

"Well, I'm going to give you some options," Ront sneered. "One, you keep telling your nasty little story about how you're so pathetic that you had to force a scared woman to do your bidding..." He paused. "And then I cut out your tongue and shove it down your throat. Two, you never touch anyone ever again with your sleazy and slimy hands, you tell me where I can find Draven, then you return to your pathetic life of being his little handmaid." Ront squinted with rage. "Your choice, bub."

"Wha' about option three?" The man grinned. "I kill you when you let me go. I then take your lil friend over there," he pointed at Lerissa. "And then I'll 'ave another story to tell. 'Ow's that soun'?"

"Option four then." Ront nodded. "I drive my dagger into his throat."

"With a quick shove into the back end of his dagger, Ront plunges his dagger deep into the man's throat. Bathing the table and Ront in blood," Mr. R described.

"Hey, Gimble," Ront turned to him.

"Y-yeah?" Gimble stuttered.

"Go grab Torinn for me? Tell him I made a bit of a mess and need his help getting some answers."

"S-sure," Gimble blinked in astonishment. "I go and get Torinn." He turned to face his brother. "Uh, Ront made a mess and would love your assistance."

"Oh boy," Torinn shook his head. "What has he done this time?"

"You get up from the table and follow Gimble through the crowd. Pushing your way through a group that has now formed around Ront," Mr. R described.

Gimble raised his hand and pointed at Ront.

"As you finally break through the crowd," Mr. R began, "you're met with the sight of a blood-spattered Ront, now holding the head of a one-eyed human man. The body slumped in the chair behind him."

"W-what did you do?" Torinn stammered.

"We had a little incident." Ront shrugged.

"And what am I supposed to do about it?" Torinn glared.

"I need you to animate the head here," Ront said, holding his hands out. "He had information I needed before he met with an untimely demise."

Torinn scrunched his face. "I see." He shook his head for a moment. "I cast Speak With Dead on the head."

"As the amulet on Torinn's chest begins to shine with the

divine arcane energy of Pelor, you all watch as the head in Ront's hands begin to move," Mr. R narrated.

"Thank you, sir!" Ront nodded to Torinn. "I move the head to Gimble's level. You need to ask the head where Draven is."

"What?" Gimble scoffed. "Why me?"

"Because it'll recognize me as a hostile," Ront explained. "I did violently murder him."

Gimble sighed. "Alright." He turned to Mr. R. "Where is Draven?"

"Draven hides behind locks and doors," the head answered.

"Where are the locks and doors the Draven hides behind?" Gimble continued.

"The locks and doors are in the shadows."

Gimble rolled his eyes. "Where are the shadows that hide the locks and doors that conceal Draven?"

"Deep in the back of the guild," the head mumbled.

"Is he here in this guild hall?" Gimble asked.

"Yes."

"What was the name of the elven woman you attacked in Sumarna?" Ront joined.

"Mathaya Turiall," the head answered. "And with that last answer, any life or animation in the head disappears, and the face falls back to its final resting form," Mr. R narrated.

Ront's shoulders slumped. "I drop the head and let it roll across the floor." He closed his eyes, drew in a long breath, and with a heavy sigh he sat back up. Rolling his shoulders and shaking his head. He sat a foot taller in his chair now. "Let's go! Thank you, Torinn."

"Please be careful!" Torinn warned.

"We will." Ront nodded.

"As the two of you part ways towards the back of the

tavern, Torinn heading back to the table, who would like to go first?" Mr. R asked.

"We do!" Ront blurted. "That'll lessen the chance of them getting themselves killed."

"Alrighty then," Mr. R said. "The two of you head into the back. Down a dark, shady corridor. At the end is another thick iron door."

"I knock." Liam tapped his fist on the table.

Knock, knock, knock... knock... knock.

"A slot in the door opens and a set of glowing yellow eyes appear through the slot," Mr. R began. "Who runs through the lotus patch in the daylight sun?" A nasal voice asked.

"He who sleeps in the rose bush in the moonlit night," Ront responded, and raised his arm to Mr. R and showed him the sharpie drawing that matched the one he drew on Gimble.

"The slot slams shut," Mr. R narrated. "You hear numerous clicking and clacking. The door swings open and you're greeted by a scrawny tabaxi woman wearing the same dark leather armor and hood that you wear." He placed a fist against his chest in a salute.

Ront returned the salute. Gimble remained there a moment before understanding the gesture and returning it.

"Welcome, brethren," the tabaxi greeted. "I am Arrow."

"I am Ront," he greeted back, bowing his head. "And this is my companion, Gimble."

"What brings you before Draven?" the tabaxi asked.

"Death's Empire," Ront answered.

Mr. R's eyes grew wide. "This way," the tabaxi said. "She leads you into the room. It's a dark room with low light and black stone floors. Very reminiscent of Jabba's palace in Star Wars." He clicked his keyboard and the image appeared.

A throne-like chair was front and center. In the throne sat a tall man with horns that curled from the front of his forehead and a crown that rested behind them. His black hood rested atop the crown. He wore the black gear like everyone else, but over his shoulder, he wore a black fur pelt.

"Who dares disturb Draven in his private chambers?" Mr. R bellowed.

"Don't you recognize me?" Ront rolled his eyes with a smile.

"Well, I'll be damned!" Draven let out a rumbling laugh. "The prodigal son returns!" He threw his arms out wide. "How've ya been, my boy?"

"It's been some time." Ront grinned embarrassedly.

"Some time?" Draven raised his eyebrow. "Boy, I haven't seen you since you were still just a child."

"Can't a guy drop in on his family every once in a long while?" Ront voice quivered.

"Only when he's here to ask for a favor," Draven sighed.

"I see I've become predictable, haven't I?" Ront shrugged.

"What do you want?" Draven's tone dropped. Almost to a disappointing level.

"I reach into my pocket and pull out the medallion I took in Kravier from Greg's minion. I toss it at his feet," Ront narrated. "I need passage to Tr'heymount."

"Okay great." Draven eyed Ront. "Why come to me? You seem to be well off without my help."

"Don't play coy with me, Uncle!" Ront groaned.

The entire table went still. Nobody moved. Nobody blinked.

"You know what that medallion means! You know what it

brings!" Ront growled. "We just took out one of their minions here in Shadestone. A kobold posing as a king."

"So what do you want from me?" Draven scowled.

"Safe passage through your trade routes." Ront sighed.

"Passage through my trade routes?" Draven grumbled. "You disappear from your family for decades, no writing, no visits, nothing, and then you barge in here demanding travel through my trade routes?" He pursed his lips tight. "I've only got one thing to say to someone like you." His lips released into a massive smile. "What else can I getcha?"

Ront and Gimble both released their shoulders with a massive sigh.

"What?" Draven asked. "Did you think I was really gonna kill my own nephew?"

"Some days, yeah." Ront laughed.

"What can I get for you both?" Draven repeated.

"Well, there's a few more than just us." Ront gave a guilty grin. "There's about six of us. And also one more favor after that." He winced.

"Anything for my sister's only son." Draven chuckled.

"I have one more companion with us. A dragonborn we freed from that kobold I mention earlier. He a marvelous fighter, but he needs a place to get back on his feet," Ront explained.

"He shall be welcomed like a brother!" Draven assured him.

"Thank you, Uncle," Ront sighed.

"But I leave you with a small stipulation," Draven said.

"I was afraid of that," Ront mumbled.

"I have a shipment going to D'thammer through the route you'll be taking," Draven began. "I will send two of my men with you all. From there they will split with you and head southwest as you go northwest. But they will leave you with another small shipment that needs to be dropped at Faria. Which happens to be on your way to Tr'heymount. Do this for me and you may use my route, horses, rations, and men."

"I want to warn you now," Ront looked at Gimble. "Last time we were in Faria, we kind of destroyed the Dragon's Tale and got wrapped up in this whole issue, to begin with."

"Well then," Draven laughed. "I guess you can make amends, too. This shipment is a special, rare, and highly illegal alcohol that just happens to be going to that very inn."

Ront rolled his eyes and stuck his hand out. Mr. R promptly threw his hand into his nephew's and shook it.

"Very well," Draven said. "I will have your caravan ready for you in the morning. Until then, relax. Take your boots off, have a drink, and some food. My boy, you look so thin. There will be plenty of room for you and your companions to rest upstairs." He motioned behind Ront. "Took! Braemar! Go ready the rooms on the third floor." Mr. R cleared his throat. "You watch as two hooded kenku rush off and out the door. Each one letting out a squawk of acknowledgment as the leave."

"Thank you." Ront bowed his head.

"Just remember," Mr. R bellowed in Draven's voice. "You are always family. We love you and will always help you. But it doesn't hurt to write or even stop by."

"Yes, Uncle," Ront replied.

"Now," Draven laughed. "Let us celebrate your return!"

"I nod and head back towards the room we left everyone in," Ront said.

"Nephew!" Draven called out. "Where are you going? You

can't leave the festivities yet. The women haven't even started dancing."

"Yes Uncle, I'm aware," Ront began.

"I start playing some music to pick up this party," Gimble interjected.

"Ah, I like your friend here, Ront." Draven chuckled. "Why leave such a grand celebration?"

"I'm going to be with my other family for a moment," Ront answered him.

"Nonsense!" Draven wailed. "I have sent my men for them. They will join us soon enough."

Ront let out a sigh. "Alright."

"Okay." Mr. R smiled. "Moving to the rest of you. You've been sitting in this sketchy tavern for what feels like hours. No one comes to serve you and almost everyone has been eyeing both your table and the bloody mess at the table across the room."

"Why don't they paint a picture?" I asked. "Make it last longer."

Ben reached over and punched my shoulder.

"What? They want to keep staring," I said, shocked that he would hit me.

"After a long while a group of hooded figures approaches your table," Mr. R continued. "Their gear, although very similar to every other being in the tavern, has slight modifications that seem to indicate higher purpose or importance amongst the guild. A scrawny tabaxi woman leads the group. Behind her, three tall and bulky figures loom." Mr. R sipped his drink. "My name is Arrow." She bowed her head.

"Great!" I blurted out. "I'll take the largest flagon of ale you've got."

Ben gave me a quick kick under the table.

"Yes," Lerissa spoke up. "What can we do for you?"

"You must come with me," Arrow replied.

"And why must we?" Torinn interrogated.

"The mighty Draven requests your presence in his chambers," Arrow hissed.

I slammed my fist down on the table. Lerissa put her hand up towards me and I calmly returned to my sitting position.

"And to what do we owe the pleasure of being requested by the great Draven?" Lerissa asked.

"At the courtesy of your companions," Arrow answered.

"Then we will come with you," Lerissa assured. She gave me a stern look and I nodded.

This look usually meant one thing. Prepare for trouble.

BREAK TIME

"And I think that is a good spot to break," Mr. R yawned. "Daryl looks like he might explode."

I looked to Daryl who was now rocking in his seat. There was a vein in his neck that looked like it was trying to escape from his skin.

"Dude, go!" Jake blurted out.

Daryl leapt from his chair and hurried towards the bathroom.

"So, Uncle Matt," Liam spoke up. "Before we break can I speed things along a little? When they meet up with me, I want to quickly explain our situation and rest for the evening."

"Alright." Mr. R nodded. "Anyone else has some quick actions they would like to pursue?"

"I continue with the festivities until it begins to die down and then I'll sneak off to rest," Jake explained.

"Me too!" I added in. "Except I'll stay with the festivities until I pass out somewhere. You know, the typical dwarf at a party."

"I'm going to turn in with Ront. Prepare my spells and such for the journey ahead of us." Laura explained.

"Since nobody was able to heal me," Ben joined. "I leave early and heal my wounds, do my meditation, then turn in." He closed his book and walked out of the room.

"I forgot that he was wounded," I said. "He didn't say anything."

"Things kind of went fast," Laura reminded me. "We went from interrogating to fleeing very quickly."

"I guess you're right." I sighed. "Well, now I feel bad for neglecting him."

"He'll be fine," Laura assured. "Let him blow off some steam. Maybe go give him a duel in a little bit. After he's had a soda and some pizza. Food tends to put his emotions back in place."

"Speaking of food," Liam said, throwing his index finger in the air. He then proceeded to pick up his plate and empty soda cans and make his way to the kitchen.

"Good idea!" I exclaimed. I followed his lead into the kitchen.

Ben was in there sulking in the corner behind a can of root beer. I made my way to him, first passing the pizza and picking up a slice from both of our boxes.

"A slice for the good sir?" I asked, offering him the plate.

He took the slice off the plate and proceeded to eat it without a word.

"So," I continued, trying to get a conversation rolling. "How about those sports-ball teams last night?"

He remained silent.

"The weather?"

Nothing.

"Dude, you can't still be that angry about the whole not-healing-you thing."

He sipped his root beer.

"Everything happened so fast," I reminded him. "There are six of us trying to figure out how to stop this evil being from destroying our world. Sometimes we just need to push past getting stabbed for a few minutes and figure out passage across the continent."

He scoffed. But a small grin grew on the side of his mouth, before he caught himself.

"Is there more to this anger than just the game?" I asked.

He closed his eyes and drew in a deep breath. He let it out with a slow sigh. "I'm fine," he finally said. "Just having some personal conflicts. I took that out on you guys but it really had nothing to do with you."

"Well, what did it have to do with?"

He pursed his lips in thought. "It's just the whole custody thing between my parents. It's got me all sorts of messed up right now." He sipped his drink. "I've always hoped that Dad would come back to be with us. But he left us. Abandoned us and forgot us. And now after all these years, he wants me to come live with him across the world?"

I sat there processing what to say. I mean what do you say to someone in this situation? I can't tell him he's lucky to have a dad. How lucky could you be when your dad doesn't care enough to be in your life? I can't tell him I know how he feels. I know my dad won't be coming back anytime soon.

"I know you understand the whole living without a dad thing." Ben sighed. "And I'm sorry if my daddy issues are awkward or upsetting to you. I know how much you wish you could have your dad show up again."

I guess that works.

"I just—" Ben stopped to think "Can't we make a deal with the Raven Queen in real life? I'll trade her my so-called father for yours?"

Man, I wish.

"Sorry," Ben apologized. "I'm making this a whole lot worse."

"No," I lied. "You're processing your emotions. It's hard to go through what you're being put through." I put my arm around his shoulder and gave him a squeeze. "Just remember what we're all here for. Our parents dump us on Mr. R for cheap therapy, while they all work so that we can one day have the lives they hope we can. I mean hell, look at Daryl." I motioned to the now-relaxed Daryl coming into the kitchen.

"What about me?" Daryl asked.

"This crazy kid is already looking at colleges, and we're not even close to graduating yet," I explained.

"Well yeah," Daryl said. "How else am I going to get ahead in this world? Juilliard doesn't just accept anyone."

"And his mom is busting her butt while he sits here and plays games with us." I laughed. "This is a healthy environment our parents built for us so we can work out our frustrations. So go ahead and process those emotions! Because afterward, we've got a lich to kill."

Ben finished the slice of pizza I brought him and washed it down with his root beer before letting out a nasty, guttural belch.

"Thanks, Jack," he said with a smile.

"So you're healed. What do you guys propose our battle plan be?" Liam broke in.

"I forgot you were in here." Ben laughed. "Guess I can't feel too angry about being forgotten now, huh?"

"I'm used to it," Liam muttered. "Anyways. Plan, we need a plan. What should we do?"

"What do you mean?" Daryl asked.

"How do we take down this powerful being?" Liam reiterated. "We managed to beat him last time and then he all of the sudden came back to consciousness and disappeared. How do we prevent him from getting away this time?"

"First off," Ben began. "This time we need to be together as a group."

"I agree," I added. "We're much stronger together."

"I think we also need another visit from Rolen the dragon again," Liam continued. "He did some work last time."

Ben nodded.

I felt my phone buzz in my pocket. I pulled it out while Liam continued strategizing.

Mom

-Hey Jackie!
    -How's the game going?
    -Anything interesting?

                       -It's goin'.
            -We met Ront's uncle!
-Now we're off to find Greg and hopefully end him for good! But we'll see in a little bit.

-Awesome!

-I can't wait to hear about it!

-BTW, do you know where the new case of Grenades went?

-Grande's*

-Grenadine!

-Damn autocorrect.

-I thought you owned a bar, not an army surplus!

-I put them on the stock shelf.

-Should be next to or behind the tequila.

-If not, check the walk-in I might have put them with the limes by accident.

-Found it!

-Was hiding behind the limes.

-Thanks, baby!

-Love you! Now go kill me a lich!

-Will do! Love you, mom!

-And sorry for hiding the Grenades!

-Grande's*

-Autocorrect hates Grenadine, doesn't it?

I put my phone back into my pocket and looked back up at everyone. Jake and Laura were now a part of the strategic planning.

"I think we need to cast as many anti-magic spells as we can," Laura suggested.

"What about our spells?" Ben asked.

"No, anti-magic that is individualized towards a single effect or spell," Liam tried to explain.

"Like what?" Daryl eyed suspiciously.

"Counterspell for starters," Jake answered. "Besides that maybe Dispel Magic, Antimagic Field, and if we get desperate we could use Banishment."

"Let's not use that last one," Ben said. "Might be a bad idea to send him to another plane that is magically more powerful or potent. That could spell disaster for us all."

"I just meant it as a last resort. Like we're badly beaten, and can't do anything more to him," Jake explained. "But I totally get what you mean."

"Can't we just bash and slash our way out?" I joked.

"I feel like if we could," Liam began. "We would have been done with him months ago."

"Well when it comes to combat with magic," I sighed. "I'm kind of caput."

"What do you mean?" Daryl glared at me. "You were spell-casting against Thray'dar. What happened to all that?"

"It was a one-time trick." I frowned. "I could get another one, but it would take a bit of gold and also would mean we'd have to go back to Dracomear again."

"That's how long you've had that?" Liam blurted out.

"The second visit, yeah." I nodded.

"And you wasted it on a gladiatorial battle?" Daryl shouted.

"Thray'dar was a strong opponent!" I argued. "I was being blasted with lightning. What else was I supposed to do?"

"That could have been useful in a desperate time," Daryl continued to berate me.

"Like when? Against Greg?" I shook my head. "The mega powerful wannabe lich?"

"Maybe," Daryl rebutted.

"That's madness!" I shot back.

"THIS—IS—SPARTA!" Liam shouted. He turned to Ben and pretended to thrust his leg into Ben's chest. In return, Ben threw himself backward in a dramatic arch of his back. Daryl glared at the two. Both who were now giggling at their own jokes.

"Either way," I said, returning the attention back to the debate. "It's gone. We don't have a low-level spell from the barbarian anymore. We need to carry on without it and find a way to destroy him."

"What if we just lock my uncle outside in the cold until he kills Greg in some freak accident?" Liam suggested.

"Interesting strategy," Mr. R chuckled. "But it won't work." He pulled out a set of keys from his pocket and gave them a jingle. "Jack's dad used to lock me out of the house all the time when we were living together. Safe to say, I have never gone without a set of house keys in my pocket since."

That sounded like Dad. He was always playing pranks on his friends, and trying to make everyone smile. Mom always talked about his casual coffee pranks. He used to have an eyeball bouncy ball that he would slip into my mom's mug when she wasn't looking. Or one year, she said he had hidden self-inflating whoopee cushions in all the furniture. She still thinks there's one or two of them hiding in the house still.

"I'm pretty sure somewhere there is a hidden prank that he left behind that I still haven't triggered," Mr. R joked.

"Knowing him you won't find it for a long while." I laughed.

"Maybe you can find it for me?" Mr. R said with a massive smile.

"I'll start looking right away!" I threw my hand up in a salute.

I felt my phone buzz in my pocket again.

Laura

-Hey! When you get the chance, check your bag!

-Hey, hey, hey! I'm the son of the prankster!

-Relax!
  -I'm not pranking you!
  -I left a present in there for you!

I looked up from my phone and eyed her. Giving her a quick up and down. She returned the stare down before giving me a wink. But for once, I didn't get spaghetti legs. I winked back at her and casually made my way back into the game room. Only stopping to grab another slice of pizza and soda.

I walked into the empty game room and set my stuff on the table. I picked up my bag and set it in my chair. I looked inside and saw a small present wrapped in Flash-themed paper. Taped to the paper was a note.

· · ·

Jack,

I know what a huge fan of this series you are! They happened to have one copy left when I went over to Brian's Comic store! He even held it aside for me knowing you'd freak to have this! So enjoy, dude!

Hugs, kisses, and all that crap,
    Your Girl, Laura!

My girl. That rang in my head as I said it again and again to myself. I turned the gift over and slid my finger under the tape holding it all together. I was meticulous that way. I liked to keep the paper intact.

I opened the top of the wrapping paper and slid the contents out. There in my hand was the one book I needed to complete my collection!

Bone: The Complete Cartoon Epic.

The entire Bone series all-in-one thirteen hundred and eighteen-page book. In its original black and white.

Growing up, I had read through my dad's collection of the comic, eventually saving up my money and buying the color versions. And now in my hands, I have finally gotten every version of the series there is.

I thumbed through the book, checking out a few pages here and there and nearly drooling as I read the mishaps and blunders of their adventure. The locust swarm that separates the three cousins. The giant bug that wants to beat up Phone Bone.

It's all there in black and white, and I couldn't be more like a kid in a candy store! I pulled out my phone to text Laura.

But something caught my eye. The box of Aunt Marisha's photography. There was a picture sticking out. I couldn't quite make out what it was. I moved closer and pulled the picture from the side of the box.

My heart sank into my stomach. I almost thought I was going to puke. This wasn't just any picture. This was the last picture taken with her Polaroid camera.

It was the picture that my mom took of the crash that killed Aunt Marisha and my dad. That killed both of Liam's parents. That put Mr. R in a wheelchair. That caused Jake to vow a lifetime of sobriety. The crash that changed our lives forever.

It was just the car surrounded by paramedics and firefighters. The destroyed front end of the Toyota 4Runner still fused and folded with the massive F-250's less-damaged front end. My dad's cut up and bloody *Mars Attacks* shirt still hanging from the little bit of windshield that's left.

I looked at the small bit in the top left corner, and my blood began to boil. My face grew hot, my arms began to tingle, and the hair on my neck stood up straight.

That was the driver of the pickup truck. His face was still bright red from how drunk he was. Mom says he was so drunk he didn't know what had happened until he woke up two days later in his holding cell.

Rich Maywell.

Just thinking his name made my jaw lock up and my muscles begin to tighten. This was the man who had killed my dad and my aunt! The man whose stupid decisions took away my only dad! This pathetic excuse for a pile of dog shit was the reason I don't get to celebrate Father's Day! The reason Mom and I lived with her parents for the majority of my childhood. Why some years during Hanukkah, Mom cried because the only gifts she could afford were clothes from Goodwill. The man who caused our mailbox to constantly overflow with bills from the hospital and the mortuary. Bills that were stamped "Past Due" or "Final Notice."

I met Rich a few times as a kid. They had brought me into the courtroom during his trial to show him what he had done. The effect his actions had on everyone else. I met him a second time when they allowed him to see Mr. R at the hospital. That was the first time we all saw Mr. R after the surgery attempt at fixing his shattered vertebrae, and the last time I saw him was a couple years ago when he had requested to see us after ten years of being locked away for quadruple vehicular manslaughter and a DUI with a blood alcohol level of point two hundred and fifty-three.

He asked to see my mom, Mr. R, Jake, Liam, and me. He wanted to see how we had been. Wanted to make sure that Liam and I had been getting the funds he'd been sending out from the work he'd done while in jail. He sobbed and apologized for what seemed like hours. Mom and Mr. R say they've forgiven him for what he has done to us., but Liam and I still hate the man to this day. He's going to rot in that cell. But you know what makes me angrier than the fact he took both my dad and my aunt? His wife was pregnant with twins at the time of the accident. He was going to be a dad, and he chose to risk his life knowing they were only weeks away!

I'd met them before they moved to another country. All I remember was feeling sorry for both of them. But also I was envious. They didn't have their father taken from them. They never met him. Their mother had met an amazing man who adopted them as his own. Last I heard from them, they were living in Switzerland. Far away from the man who could have easily ruined their lives as much as he did to us.

I could feel the massive knot that was in my throat. It was nearly impossible to swallow. My eyes began to burn from the tears as they filled my eyes. The tears were almost relieving as they ran down my warm cheeks. I wiped my sleeve across my face.

The anger and sorrow chased around in my chest. Like a tornado throwing me left and right. I couldn't process which emotion I should feel. But in a final moment of weakness and utter pain. I collapsed to my knees and just wept.

It felt like everything inside of me had broken. By the time I finished sobbing, my eyes were beyond dry and puffy. My nose was raw and tender, and I just sat there in an emotionless void. I had very little energy to move. But I was startled by a sudden hand on my shoulder.

I spun around to see Mr. R sitting behind me with streaks of tears running down his cheeks. He hoisted himself from his chair and carefully sat down on the ground beside me. He took the picture from my hands and tore it up. He looked back to me and held his arms out.

I collapsed in his chest. An emotional pile of teenager. He wrapped his arms around me and held me tight.

"I'm so sorry, kiddo," Mr. R choked out. "I've been searching for that picture for years now. I never, ever, ever wanted it to end up with you or Liam. I wanted to destroy it. I'm so sorry."

I sniffed and cleared my throat, but nothing came out as I tried to speak.

We sat there for a couple more minutes before he shifted towards the box and pulled out another picture.

"Now this is the picture I also wanted to find." Mr. R laughed as he handed me the picture.

It was everyone in the picture. Mom, Dad, Liam's parents, and Jake standing behind Ben and Laura's Mom, Mr. R stood off to the side. Between Mr. R and Jake was a mirror. In the reflection stood Aunt Marisha and her camera.

I couldn't help but laugh at their ingenuity. But it worked! Everyone was accounted for in the picture.

"She was crazy smart like that," Mr. R chuckled. "Your aunt could always figure a way to make things work. One of her many qualities that I loved about her, and one of her many qualities that you seem to have, too." He let out a sigh. "But that's all in the past now. It's time to move forward." He patted me on the back and began to shuffle back into his chair. "You all have a powerful magic user to destroy."

I blinked the residual tears out of my eyes and got to my feet. I shook my arms and ran in place for a moment. Then I stood there for a moment, taking a deep breath to clear my head. I turned around back to the box of photos and cameras, picked out the digital Nikon. I took off the shutter cover and clicked through the auto-focusing lens.

Mr. R wheeled out of the room and into the kitchen, returning moments later, followed by everyone else.

"So you'll go with me?" Daryl asked Liam.

"Yeah, why not? I think it's time to let my red and black deck stretch its legs. I haven't played a Magic tournament in forever." Liam laughed.

"Black and red?" Ben scoffed. "That'll be no match against Jack's blue and white deck."

I chuckled. Totally forgot about the tournament tomorrow. But that didn't matter right now.

As everyone took their seat, I pulled the camera to my eye, waited for the lens to focus, and snapped a picture with everyone in it. Making sure that I was in the reflection of the mirror on the shelf behind Laura.

I examined the picture on the LED screen, turned the camera off and set it on the table. I moved my binder in front of me, opening it to my character sheet.

"Alright." Mr. R smiled. "Let us continue."

PILGRIMAGE

"You all wake the following morning, refreshed and revived," Mr. R began. "As you all slowly make your way into the tavern proper, you're met by the scene of passed-out assassins, thieves, and mercenaries; a grand army of rogues drunkenly asleep in a tavern. A faint smell of breakfast wafts into the room from the kitchen, and eventually fills the tavern, as carts are wheeled in and set up buffet style." He leaned on the table. "I suggest you lot get some of this before they all wake up." He grinned.

"I take his advice!" I blurted out.

"You all bear witness to your dwarven companion as he begins piling high a mound of food on his now-hidden plate." Mr. R laughed. "Making his way through the eggs and sausage, he stops at the bacon and packs a nice serving onto his already massive meal. You see the chef's eyes grow wider as he watches Adrik shove disks of blood pudding in his mouth and on his plate."

"Dude." Ront shook his head. "Save some for the rest of us!"

I snorted at him with a laugh. "And miss out on any of this spread? Yeah right!"

"I follow behind him in the plate-stacking contest," Gimble blurted.

"After commenting on Adrik's plate piling skills, Gimble comes up behind him with a plate almost as tall as Adrik's. But instead of blood pudding in his mouth, Gimble is balancing a stack of buns on his head," Mr. R depicted. "You hear the chef mumble under his breath, *Maybe I should go make more food.*"

Ront shook his head and rolled his eyes. He then gestured to Torinn, Rolen, and Lerissa to come get food.

"Are you not eating, Ront?" Torinn asked.

"Not that hungry." Ront sighed. "But don't worry about me. Eat and enjoy. We've got quite the trek ahead of us."

"Have you taken this trip before?" Lerissa questioned.

"A long time ago." Ront smiled. "When I was still merely learning the family business."

"Speaking of the family business," Mr. R said in a familiar bellowing voice. "Once you are all finished with your breakfast, I have your caravan all packed and ready to set out on the trail."

"And I'm guessing that means the cargo is loaded on there, too?" Ront asked.

"It is being loaded as we speak," Draven assured. "Now come, my nephew, eat, enjoy, be merry!" He put his hand on his nephew's shoulder. "Enjoy this time we have together as a family," he said somberly.

"Thank you, Mr. Draven," I said with a mouth full of food.

"Yeah, thanks," Gimble echoed.

"Of course my friends!" Draven's voice boomed again. "Anything for the heroes of Shadestone."

"Heroes?" Lerissa choked. Laura coughed on the soda she was swallowing.

"Well of course." Draven laughed. "You lot have caught the public eye for the good you did yesterday. Not only did you take down the self-proclaimed 'king', but you also scared the other blokes who follow Greg's empire, out of the city. The people are raving about what you've done for us."

"You're kidding?" Rolen questioned.

"I'm not." Draven smiled. "You all have done us a great service. And for your help, I offer you my aid whenever you need it. If you're ever in a bind, just find the symbol," He held up his arm and revealed the symbol on his wrist. "And tell them I sent you. Now I apologize for this part." Draven winced. "You all feel hands grab your wrists, followed by a searing pain," Mr. R narrated. "And when the hands release, you all have a black, swollen marking embedded in your skin. Draven's symbol."

"Really?" Gimble groaned. "I had to do that twice."

"Sorry." Ront shrugged. "Didn't think they would mark you guys."

Gimble frowned, "I'd better get—"

"I take his wrist and cast Cure Wounds on the one Ront carved," Torinn interrupted.

"I guess that works." Gimble shrugged.

"Alright." Ront shook his head. "We need to get moving. The more time we waste here, the more powerful Greg becomes."

"I feel like at this point, no matter how strong he is, it's not going to change the fact one of us, if not all, are going to die," Rolen noted.

"Hey!" I blurted out through another mouthful of food. "Always look on the bright side of life."

Gimble and Torinn proceeded to follow that with the whistling tune from Monty Python's *Life of Brian*.

Rolen shook his head. "I'm serious. Also, to make matters worse, he's still got Elfi and Ashear."

"So let's get going," Ront repeated himself.

"Yes," Mr. R bellowed in Draven's voice again. "You all should get moving. If not for your sake, then do it for the sake of the guild."

"I move towards the back room," Liam directed. "You lot coming?"

"I follow him," Laura said.

"Me too," Ben followed.

"I go after Rolen," Daryl explained.

"I guess we'd better go." Gimble laughed. "I hand my plate over to the chef, take the rolls off my head, and place all but one back on the buffet, and dart off behind the group."

I let out a deep, annoyed sigh. "I get up with my plate in hand. I walk up to the chef, take Gimble's plate from him, and follow everyone else."

"With two plates in your hands?" Mr. R raised his eyebrow.

"Yes," I answered through another mouthful of food.

I looked up just in time to catch Laura's gaze. She was giggling at my humor. Like tears from the corners of her eyes giggling. I could feel the blood rushing to my cheeks. My facial heat intensifying, I had to have been as red as tomato.

"You all make your way through the back of the tavern, into Draven's throne room, and out a back door, ending up in a small alleyway," Mr. R narrated. "When you come out you're met by a large wagon. It's so big, it almost seems impossible to have fit in the alley. But walking in and out of the wagon is a group of halflings. Some are just coming out, while others team-carry wooden crates that are clanking and jingling with glass." He took a sip from his drink. "And then you're all approached by a tall elven man. Standing eye to eye with Ront, the thin man towers over the two halflings of your party, while looming over the other three normal-sized beings of your group, his pale, white skin almost glowing against the black hood over his silver hair."

Mr. R clicked his keyboard and the elven man appeared on the screen. Mr. R raised his chin up towards the sky. "So you are the... heroes?" The elf sneered.

"And you are...?" I quipped, my mouth still full of food.

Mr. R glared at me. "My name, dwarf, is Varis. And you are...?"

I jammed my thumb in my chest. "My name is Adrik of clan Frostbeard. Defenders of crown Baldrick. Heir to the throne of the Ancient King Baern," I listed off.

"Well, your highness." Varis rolled his eyes. "I come from the kingdom of Galanodel, so excuse me if I seem bitter at the presence of a Baldrick. And the rest of you?"

"I'm Ront, nephew of Draven," Ront proclaimed. He turned his gaze to me. Then returned it to Varis. "And Adrik here is my companion and lifelong friend. Any petty quarrel you have with him, you have with all of us."

"My apologies." Varis bowed his head.

"Pick your head up," Ront demanded. "I may be Draven's nephew, but I am no king. This journey you have with us will be short. I do not expect you to follow any of my commands, as I hope there will be none. But, I expect cooperation between both parties until our paths separate. Are these terms agreeable?"

"Quite agreeable." Varis nodded. "If we are closing formalities early then," he gestured behind himself. "These are my men." Mr. R clicked his keyboard. In front of Varis, two identical halflings appeared on the screen. Wearing the similar black hoods, one had a bow and quiver across his back, while the other had a lute across hers.

"Meet Arila and her brother Elton," Varis introduced.

"Nice to meet you both," Gimble said, throwing his hand out. "I put my hand out to the lady first."

"The bardic woman shakes your hand," Mr. R narrated.

"Hello." Gimble grinned. "What have we here?"

"Don't flatter yourself." She laughed at him. "Elton will murder you if you get any ideas."

Gimble chuckled. "Maybe my charm will change his mind—"

"You feel a dagger press into your back," Mr. R interrupted. "Step away from my sister, bard," Elton whispered.

"Your sister is the bard," Gimble responded.

"Now!" Elton raised his voice.

Gimble threw his hands up. "Okay, okay. Maybe later."

"Now," Mr. R said in his dry Varis voice. "Shall we begin our journey?"

"Let's get going," Rolen instructed. "I've got someone to save."

"And what realm does the half-elf hail from?" Varis questioned.

"Xiloscent," Rolen said shortly. "I pass him and climb onto the wagon."

"Very well. Now," Varis continued. "Shall we carry—"

"Eh-hem," Lerissa interrupted.

"May I help you?" Varis asked.

"You're just going to skip over the two of us?" Lerissa questioned, gesturing between Torinn and herself.

"Well, I didn't really want to meet any of you," Varis sighed. "But since we are this far." He rolled his hand in a circle.

"Well," Torinn coughed out. "My name is Torinn Yarjerit. Cleric to the matron of life and light. Defender of Dracomear. Slayer of Balasar the Red. The architect of the Temple of Pelor in Dracomear. Father to Kriv, Paladin to the matron of life—"

"I get it," Varis rolled his eyes. "You have a lot of titles. You." He pointed to Lerissa. "Who are you?"

"I am—" Lerissa started.

"Keep it under five words," Varis demanded.

"—Lerissa," She finished.

"Good," Varis said. "Now can we get a move on please?"

"I'm already climbing into the wagon," Lerissa directed.

"Let's go," Ront commanded.

"You all clamber onto the wagon," Mr. R began. "It's not an ideal situation for travel. But it beats having to walk there or expend a spell slot." He looked around at the group. "Does anyone do anything important during the travels?"

Nobody said anything.

"Alright, it's a quiet journey. Few words are spoken between the party. You finally reach a large clearing along the trail." Mr. R clicked his keyboard. The image of a campsite appeared. A small fire and a couple of tents around it. The starry sky is illuminated by the bright moon overhead. "Do you join Varis in setting up a camp?"

"I have a better idea," Gimble smirked. "*Nor need we*

power or splendor, wide hall or lordly dome. The good, the true, the tender, these form the wealth of home," he recited. "And I cast Magic Mansion on the side of our wagon."

"Sarah Hale?" Ben asked.

"The one and only." Jacob laughed.

"You all listen as Gimble recites his poem of home, the arcane powers from his hands sparkle and shimmer. The door on the wagon begins to glisten with a similar arcane energy," Mr. R described.

"I open the door and walk inside," Gimble said.

"Opening the door, you expose the lush interior of your arcane mansion. Astral servants awaiting your command," Mr. R narrated.

"What are Varis and the twins doing?" Rolen asked.

"Varis is attempting to start a fire. Arila and Elton are putting up tents around said fire," Mr. R explained.

"I'm going to go over to them," Rolen said. "I'll cast Druid-craft on the fire to get it started for him."

"You wave your hand over the tinder and wood pile at your feet. A small bit of light flickers from inside the pile, quickly growing into a small campfire," Mr. R narrated.

"I move myself to a safe distance from the fire," Rolen explained. "Where I can still be warmed by the fire. But the smoke rises above me and doesn't stick in my eyes. I'm going to pop a squat in the dirt and meditate."

"You take your seat in the dirt. The energies of nature flowing through you. Almost like electricity coursing through your body," Mr. R began. "It's been awhile since you last connected with the earth. You can feel the world around you, almost like it's breathing. You feel the slow and steady growth of the trees, the gentle push and pull of the current in the small lake little ways down the trail. You sense the prairie dogs burrowing for the evening. You even feel the breathing patterns and heartbeat of Varis."

"I'm going to go sit with Rolen by the fire," Ront said. "Connect with the Raven Queen."

"I follow suit," Torinn added.

"You both move over to the now crackling fire. Kneeling beside your companion," Mr. R explained. "Describe to me what you both choose to do."

Ront gestured to Torinn.

"I take my mace and place it in the dirt behind us," Torinn began. "I then kneel beside Rolen. I remove my amulet and place it on the ground in front of me. I close my eyes. In my chest, I trigger my fire breath to warm and illuminate my throat, and releasing the smoke through my nose."

Mr. R nodded, then turned his attention to Ront.

"I kneel on the other side of Rolen. I take out the Raven dagger and place it in front of me on the ground," Ront explained. "I try to match my breathing pattern to these two." He pointed at Rolen and Torinn.

"Alright. Lerissa and Adrik," Mr. R said, pointing at us. "You're my only two left. What's your plan for the night?"

"I would like to make my way into the mansion and just rest through the night," Lerissa answered.

"I think I'm going to go over to the fire and take a seat with these guys," I explained.

"Well hell!" Gimble blurted. "If everyone wants to party outside, I'll come sit at the fire with you guys."

"I'm still going to go in," Lerissa said. "Keep it open for me, please."

"You okay?" I asked her.

"I will be." She smiled. "I just, I need a little bit to prepare for tomorrow."

"But we're going to Faria tomorrow," I reminded her. "The fight with Greg is still another day's travel after that."

"I know," she assured me. "I just—I just think I'd be best to turn in and check my spell book."

"Alright." I nodded. "But hey, you let me know if somethin' bothering you, 'ight?"

She nodded.

"Alright," I smiled. "See you in the mornin'?"

"See you in the morning," She smiled back.

"I go and join the guys," I said.

"As you reconvene with the rest of your party around the fire, you calmly listen to the chirping of the crickets and the soft tune being played by Arila," Mr. R narrated.

"I join her," Gimble added.

"The soft tune of Arila and Gimble," Mr. R corrected.

"Do I notice anything about our companions? Heart rates? Breathing pattern?" Rolen asked.

"Nothing that seems out of ordinary," Mr. R explained. "Elton seems to be at a slightly higher heart rate than the rest. But it feels more like he's just angry."

"Alright," Rolen nodded. "And Varis, what do I feel from him?"

"He is very still. His breathing is slow," Mr. R described. "He almost feels like he's sleeping. But being the son of an elf, you know that elves don't sleep. He's in a meditative state. As you search for him some more, you begin to notice that his mind feels like it's on, racing through thought after thought."

"I'll stop snooping after that," Rolen said.

"Any of you five want to do anything else?" Mr. R asked.

"I would like to take out my sharpening stone and run it along my blade for a little bit," I explained. "Give my axe an edge again."

"Okay," Mr. R nodded. "Lerissa," He pointed his pencil at her. "What does your night look like?"

"Once I enter my chambers, I go over to my desk and stare at my spell book," Lerissa explained. "I look up at my collection of scrolls." She swished her cheeks back and forth. "I take out the key that hangs around my neck."

Ront and I exchanged looks of confusion and concern.

"I take the key and open the small locked drawer atop the shelves," she continued.

"The small black skeleton key clicks the lock into place." Mr. R explained. "The small drawer pops open."

"I slide it out and set it on my desk." Laura narrated. "I click open the second lock. Stabbing my hand on the sharp needle that pokes out from the box."

"The needle pricks your hand, drawing a single drop of deep crimson from your palm. As the blood is absorbed into the needle," Mr. R paused. "A series of clicking travels through the box. Click, click, click. Until the top lid flies open."

"I reach inside and pull out the single scroll from inside," Lerissa explained. "I hold it in my hands."

"You hold this scroll close to your chest. Feeling the arcane presence it holds. The last remnants of your mother's memory tightly gripped in your hands," Mr. R narrated. "Will you roll me a perception check?"

Laura eyed him for a moment but rolled as asked. "Fifteen."

"As you're focused on the scroll and your mother's arcane seal fills your heart, you hear your staff fall over to the floor," Mr. R depicted.

"Does it seem like it was unnatural?" Laura asked. "The way it fell, that is."

"You feel like it was. It was propped up in a spot where falling naturally was unlikely, however not impossible." Mr. R explained. "Maybe a draft caused it to fall."

"Hmm," She hummed. "I move and pick it up off the floor and set it on my bed."

"Give me a strength check," Mr. R requested.

Again she eyed him suspiciously. But still did as he asked. "Eleven?"

"When you pick up the staff, it feels heavier for a moment. Like it's being weighed down or a magnet is pulling on it."

"Before I set it down I give it a twirl. Checking the weight on it."

"It feels normal again. The usual top-heavy staff."

"I cast Light from the orb in the top of my staff," Lerissa said.

"The orb begins to glow a yellowish, white light from its center," Mr. R explained.

"Okay," she said slowly. "I set the staff down and move back to my scroll on my desk."

"Give me another perception check," Mr. R asked.

"Seventeen," Laura announced.

"You watch as your staff rolls off your bed., Mr. R narrated. "It falls to the floor again."

Laura squinted at Mr. R. "I move to my desk, hiding the box under my robes, I slip the scroll into my sleeve. Then I close the box, put it in the drawer slot, and lock it." She stopped. "And I leave the key on my desk."

"The box clicks back into the slot, locking in place," Mr. R described. "The torchlight on the walls flickers as the flames sputter at a slight breeze that blows past them."

"I lean over to pick up my staff," Laura narrated. "Slowly and carefully. I examine my staff before standing back up with it."

"Give me another perception check," Mr. R asked again.

"Fifteen," Laura responded.

"As you slowly pick your staff back up from the ground, you hear a faint sound of something dragging across the wood of your desk," Mr. R narrated.

"I spin around and cast Hold Monster!" Laura blurted out.

"As you spin around, your staff's orb now glowing with a swirling yellow energy, you are met by the sight of a small fey creature. This creature's skin is a blackish-blue. Its wide eyes, a vibrant yellow, are staring back at you in fear," Mr. R depicted. "The creature's body seems to be coming out of the small picture frame on your desk. Its long, bony fingers pinching the skeleton key between the tips."

"What are you?" Lerissa glared.

"Me no do it," Mr. R squealed in his best Gollum impression. "Me no steal key from the lady."

"Then why does *me* have *my* key between *their* fingers?" Lerissa interrogated.

"Me called Oggie." The creature explained. "Oggie is boggle."

"And what's a boggle?" Lerissa questioned, a look of confusion on her face.

"Oggie is!" He jammed his thumb in his chest. "Oggie is boggle! Oggie no from here."

"I could have told you that." Lerissa sighed. "Why are you in my room, Oggie? Why are you taking my key?"

"Oggie no wants to be," the boggle whined. "But Oggie has to!"

"Well, Oggie." Lerissa rolled her eyes. "I don't want you to take that either. So why do you *have* to take it?"

"Master says so," Oggie mumbled.

"And who is master?" Lerissa interrogated.

"No, no, no." Oggie grimaced. "Oggie no can tell."

"Come on Oggie, you can trust me."

"No," Oggie clipped. "Master no happy if Oggie tell."

"Master won't know," Lerissa tried to assure.

"No!" Oggie snapped. "Master will hurt Oggie."

"Well, Oggie," Lerissa said dryly. "If you don't tell me who wants my scroll here." She held up her hand. "Then I'm going to do the same to get the answers from you."

"No! Don't hurt Oggie!" The boggle pleaded. "Oggie just want to go home. Oggie wants home!"

"Then let me help you, Oggie." Lerissa offered. "I can send you home. Just tell me who wants my scroll, and then you will be free to go home."

Oggie's face shifted through many emotions trying to process the offer. Fear, anger, sorrow, confusion. "Master name is Greg." Oggie sighed.

"And what does he want with my scroll?"

"Oggie no know."

"Does he know what it is?"

"Master tell Oggie not to read. Said scroll dangerous."

"So he does know," Lerissa whispered to herself.

"Send Oggie home now?" Oggie begged.

"Yeah, let's get you home." Lerissa nodded.

HANGING OMENS

"I WANT TO TAKE OGGIE OUT OF THE MANSION WITH ME and go find Rolen," Lerissa explained.

"Alright." Mr. R nodded. He cleared his throat and took a sip from his drink. "As you drop Hold Monster, you watch the boggle's arm shrink in length. Matching the normal length of his other arm. He then proceeds to pull himself out of the picture frame on your desk. He carefully stretches his limbs until his feet set themselves on the ground. Like a slow slinky, his body catches up with his feet. At regular length, the boggle stands no more than three feet tall."

"I put my hand out for him to take so I can guide him through the mansion to Rolen," Lerissa explained.

"His beady yellow eyes look you up and down, examining your gesture," Mr. R narrated.

"It's okay, put your hand in mine and I'll take you home," Lerissa assured the boggle.

"You watch as he decides what to do in this moment. Unsure of whether it's safe or not," Mr. R explained.

"Don't worry, Oggie," Lerissa said. "I won't hurt you."

"With a sigh, Oggie places his hand on yours," Mr. R continued. "Lerissa, make me a wisdom saving throw."

"Son of a—" Laura cursed. She rolled. Her shoulders drooped. She held up her hand with her index finger extended out. "It's a plus eleven modifier. But it was also a critical fail." She sighed.

"As Oggie places his hand into yours, you feel a jolt of dark arcane power surge through your body. A cloud of darkness clouds your vision. Your entire body locks up with total paralysis, sending you down to the hard ground," Mr. R narrated. "'You hear Oggie's panicked voice. No! No! Master is not happy!" Mr. R cleared his throat. "And you hear the clapping of his feet against the stone floor."

"Can I fight it?" Laura asked.

"You try to, but you can't move. Your brain tells your arms to move, but nothing happens," Mr. R explained.

"Can I cry out?"

"You feel your vocal cords pull and stretch as you try to scream. But no noise is made," Mr. R narrated. "But you feel a presence. Something, almost swimming behind you. Like you're in a void and something is circling you." Mr. R clicked his keyboard and the entire room went dark.

He clicked it again and the screen in the table began to illuminate with a swirling black and green smoke.

"Lerissa." A voice echoed through the room. "Lerissa."

"Who's there?" Lerissa called out.

"Lerissa!" The voice shouted. "Come to Faria, Lerissa!" The voice growled. "Leave them here! Come to Faria!"

"Why?" Lerissa asked. "What's there for me? Nothing but pain and misery. Why should I listen to you?"

"If you don't," the voice said calmly, "your friends will perish."

Mr. R clicked his keyboard again. One by one each of our character's images flashed on the screen. Each one facing a separate doom. Decay, disease, mutilation, and hunger. Each image flashed followed by our voices.

"Lerissa! Lerissa!" We cried out through the speakers.

This was pure nightmare fuel.

"What do you want?" Lerissa shouted back.

"Come to Faria!" The voice hissed. "Abandon them! Join me in Faria!"

"What's in Faria? Why go there?" Lerissa continued to shout.

"Eternal Glory," the voice whispered.

Then the lights came back up and the screen went back to the campsite.

"Your vision comes back to you," Mr. R spoke up. "Regaining control of your body, you sit up. The mansion is still there. The servants float along the corridors as if nothing is wrong."

"Where's Oggie?" Lerissa asked.

"He's nowhere to be found, as far as you're aware," Mr. R answered.

Lerissa cursed under her breath. "I get up and run out of the mansion trying to see if I can catch him."

"You hop to your feet and barrel through the mansion. Left, right, left, left, right," Mr. R narrated. "Passing through the astral images of servants and ducking under floating objects.

You burst through the front entrance into the cold evening. Oggie is still nowhere to be found."

"You okay?" Rolen asked.

"There—a boggle—Greg—" Lerissa panted.

"Slow down," Ront joined in. "One more time. Slowly."

"There was a boggle in the mansion. In my room!" Lerissa recapped. "Greg sent him to steal—" She caught herself. "To steal me," she lied. "And when the boggle failed to take me, I had one of those 'visions.' The ones where Greg threatens everyone."

"Why is it always in my mansion?" Gimble groaned. "An arcane safe haven."

"Well, what did he want?" Torinn asked.

"He wants me to go to Faria," Lerissa sighed.

"You're kidding me?" Ront blurted out. "That means he's there! Waiting for us!"

"I'm not sure." Lerissa shook her head.

"Not sure?" Rolen raised his eyebrow. "He told you to meet him there, didn't he?"

"No," Lerissa snapped. "He said to come to Faria."

"Well, why would he send you there if not to be there to make sure you show?" I asked.

"Good point," Torinn agreed.

"What's the matter?" Varis interjected.

"Personal matters," Ront clipped.

"Well it sounds like it affects me and my people," Varis argued. "So I would like some insight."

"I'll give you insight," I threatened.

"Adrik," Ront eyed me. "This matter won't affect any of you, Varis. You will be far south before it affects us."

"Does it affect your shipment?" Varis continued to question.

"No," Ront answered.

Varis glared at Ront for a moment. "Very well." Mr. R looked across the group. "And with that, Varis walks back to his tent."

"What are we going to do?" Rolen asked.

"What can we do?" Torinn responded.

"First off," Ront sighed. "We're not letting Riss go by herself to Faria. This is one hundred and ten percent a trap. But we are better off walking into a trap with all six rather than send one."

"What do you think we should do?" Rolen repeated his question. "We can't all walk up into Faria with her. He'll kill us all the minute he sees us."

"And he's too powerful for us to attempt an ambush," Torinn added.

"An ambush?" I perked up.

"I said no ambush," Torinn reminded me. "He'd see it coming!"

"But what if he couldn't see?" I asked. "What if this ambush wasn't a typical ambush?"

"What're you getting at?" Ront raised his eyebrow.

"What if our ambush wasn't visible?" I thought. "We have multiple magic users in our midst, right? Ones who could teleport us, right?"

"You want to teleport an ambush into Faria?" Gimble questioned.

"Exactly!" I said. "We send in Lerissa alone, like he wants, maybe with one of us with her. Probably invisible. From there, the rest of the party waits for a signal just outside of the town.

Once the signal is triggered, Gimble teleports everyone into the town. Taking Greg by surprise!"

Rolen hummed with skepticism. "I don't know—"

"That might actually work!" Ront interrupted. "It might be just crazy enough to work!"

"You can't be serious?" Rolen argued.

"Think about it," Ront continued. "We send Lerissa by herself. Greg will be so distracted by the fact she's alone, he's going to try and see past her ruse. But we won't be anywhere close to him. He's too focused on trying to find the ambush we catch him off guard and take him down!"

"You're insane!" Rolen continued to protest. "We're talking about the man who can attack us from our dreams like Freddy Kruger! What makes you think that we could come close to an idea like that?"

"Well, what other ideas do you have?" Lerissa asked.

Rolen pursed his lips in thought. You could almost smell the gears grinding in his head.

"I've got nothing," he sighed. "It's the best we can come up with, I guess."

"Alright, we need to prepare for this then," Ront began. "We need to inventory our potions, prepare the spells we need, sharpen our blades, and attune our best armor!"

Rolen let out a sigh of defeat.

"I take off for the mansion!" Ront directed.

"I follow," Torinn joined.

Rolen looked at me. "Are you sure about this plan?"

"No," I admitted. "But what more can we do? We need to stop him."

"As you say this," Mr. R interrupted. "You hear a screech from the wagon."

"I hurry off to investigate!" Rolen said.

"We're right behind you!" Lerissa shouted.

"As you approach the front side of the wagon, give me a perception check," Mr. R asked.

"Eighteen?" Ben claimed.

"As you approach the wagon, you notice a black goo-like substance smeared across the sides of the wagon's chassis." Mr. R narrated. "It takes the form of a struggle to move. Handprints smeared across the goo."

"I follow the goo and the signs of struggle," Rolen continued.

"You follow the trail around to the backside of the wagon. On the ground lays a dead boggle. His stomach slashed open and the thick, black ooze seeping out of the wound." Mr. R described.

"Oggie!" Lerissa cried.

"What happened?" Rolen mumbled.

"Who's Oggie?" I asked.

"He was the boggle Greg sent to steal from—take me!" Lerissa explained. "I tried to help him! I tried to save him!"

"And it looks like Greg found out," Rolen frowned.

Tears began to trickle down Lerissa's face. "I did this to him."

"No, you didn't!" I reminded her. "You tried to help him get away! How were you to know that Greg was going—could even do this to him?"

Her eyes were now red and puffy from the tears.

"But—"

"No buts!" I cut her off. "No cuts! No coconuts!"

Lerissa shook her head and smiled through the tears. "You're right." She wiped away the tears from her eyes.

"This just means that a-hole has to pay double now!" I told her.

"We better get inside," Rolen warned. "Before we come to the same fate as Oggie."

"I scoop up Oggie's body," Lerissa began. "And I want to take him over to the campfire." She sniffled. "Rolen, can you grow the branches a little bigger so I can set him on them?"

Rolen scrunched his nose in contemplation. "Sure," He finally said. "I use Druidcraft and make a small bed over the fire for her to lay him in."

"You all watch, with a wave of Rolen's hand, the blackened branches in the fire pit begin to grow and intertwine with each other into a small bed shape." Mr. R depicted.

"I carefully lay him on the bed of branches," Lerissa sighed through more tears. "I want to cast Prestidigitation and make his body presentable for his final moments."

"As the arcane energy swirls from your hand and around Oggie's still body, you watch as the wounds begin to close. The black blood stains fade from his midnight blue skin. His beaten face looks untouched and has a small smile on it." Mr. R narrated.

"I cast Firebolt at the base of the branch bed," Lerissa whispered.

"With a small spark of flame from your hand, the lower portion of the branches ignite. Slowly rising and engulfing the bed." Mr. R described.

"Final cantrip," Lerissa choked through tears. "I cast Message to the three in the mansion." She moved her hand to her ear. "Will you guys come back outside for me? We're having a funeral and require the presence of the gods. And some music to guide them along."

"Who died—" Torinn began to ask. But Gimble put his hand up to stop him. They nodded to each other in understanding.

"We're on our way," Gimble responded.

"As the three of you walk out of the mansion and off the wagon. You're met with the scene of a cremation. Adrik, Lerissa, and Rolen standing over the now burning body." Mr. R narrated.

Ront closed his eyes and drew in a deep breath. When he opened them, he looked to Torinn who nodded.

"Torinn and I—" Ront choked out. "Torinn and I move to both ends of the body."

"I take my medallion off my neck and hold it in my hands," Torinn began. "I hold it above my head." He raised his hands up and closed his eyes.

"I do the same with my dagger," Ront added.

"I pull out my violin," Gimble joined. Jake got up out of his chair and moved over to one of the shelves behind Ben and Daryl. He reached up to the top shelf, above the miniatures, and pulled down a violin and the bow to go with it. "My apologies," He laughed. "It's been a while." He blew the dust off the top and gave it a few plucks to tune. He turned the pegs. Placing the violin on his shoulder, he took in a breath and began playing softly.

It took him a couple seconds to figure out what he was doing. But once he found his fingerings, he was playing a lovely version of *Wish You Were Here* by Pink Floyd.

"A life cut short by the powers of evil, your sacrifice shall not be in vain." Ront began to recite.

"From the light of the goddess of life," Torinn joined.

"And the shadows of the matron of death."

"We free you from your mortal bonds. And guide you to the next plane, where you may rest your weary soul."

"Your chains of mortality are broken," Ront raised his voice.

"Go forth unto the light!" Torinn choked out.

"Requiescat in pace," Ront sighed.

"You all watch as the boggle's body continues to burn and crumble into ashes. As the last remnants of structure to his body fall to the heat, the flames begin to change colors." Mr. R began to describe. "Circling colors of blue, green, and purple. The colors of an aurora in the northern skies. Ront. Torinn. As the flames change color, so does your presence on this plane. The rest of you watch as the paladin and cleric's eyes begin to glow. Torinn's a bright white light. Ront's a misty black."

Mr. R clicked his keyboard and the screen went dark.

"You both feel your presence pulled from their place on the material plane." Mr. R continued. "Suspended into a black and white void." he clicked his keyboard and the black screen was cut in half with bright white.

Slowly emerging onto the screen were two women. One dressed in black and feathers on the white side. Dark flowing hair contrasting her pale skin. A white mask in her hand. On the other half, a blonde woman floating in a white gown. Her skin a golden tan. In the middle of her gown, a golden sun with wavy rays almost seem to shine off the screen. The two women a contrast to the other. The two women representing life and death. Pelor and the Raven Queen.

"You have brought forth a being of noble heart. The two women say in unison," Mr. R said. "But his actions of evil intent."

"Yes, Your Graciousness," Torinn bowed his head.

"His life, corrupted by the evil of our enemy," the goddess' continued. "Why do you bring a pawn of this evil to us?"

"Your holiness," Ront spoke up. "We bring him before you as a glimpse into those affected by this evil. A creature who was only doing what would hopefully keep him alive. All he wanted was to survive. As all we mortals do."

"But in his actions of good heart and faith, he paid the ultimate sacrifice." Torinn sighed. "Greg ended this creature's life out of anger and out of hatred. He lived his last moments in fear of what they would—No, what they did do to him!"

"Why does he deserve our forgiveness?" The women asked.

"He was no more evil than you or I," Ront pleaded.

"He had done no wrong. Even in his final moments!" Torinn added.

"We ask of you to take this being with forgiveness," Ront took a deep breath. "In return, I offer you my second life."

"What're you doing—" Torinn tried asking. But Ront just put his hand up.

"And why would we desire your life in return for our forgiveness of another?" The gods questioned.

"Because you don't want to repeat your past by granting me an eternal existence like you did with Greg and Froug." Ront reminded them. "You both fear of what I will become if I were to survive the coming battle. You fear that I might see what Greg stands for. That I would turn against you both, using the gift you granted me!"

The gods eye him for a moment.

"This guarantees an end to your fears," Ront continued. "I promise you my soul for eternity if you give this creature forgiveness and guidance into the next plane."

Torinn stared in awe at his companion.

"We shall accept the terms which you set forth," the goddesses agreed. "We agree to your servitude for the forgiveness of the boggle creature named Oggie."

"As you wish," Ront bowed his head.

"But before we send you back, we offer you a gift." Mr. R filed through his binder and pulled out two laminated index cards. "Take these into battle with you."

"Why give us these?" Torinn asked. "Why not come and fight by our side?"

"We can no longer interfere in the dealings of man." The gods answered.

"But this all began with you interfering," Torinn reminded them.

"In time, all will be explained!" The women said. "For now, go back to your realm. Defeat this evil. Bring balance back to the world!"

Mr. R clicked his keyboard and between the goddesses appeared a smiling boggle. His sharp yellow teeth peeking from behind his dark blue lips.

"You both watch as the gods turn and escort Oggie off into the void, fading from existence." Mr. R narrated. "You both suddenly feel like you're falling as you're both thrown back into your bodies once more!" He clicked the keyboard again and the campsite appeared.

"Are you both okay?" I asked.

"It's been done," Ront nodded with a smile. "Oggie has made it to the other side."

"Oh thank you both!" Lerissa cheered. "I run over and pull them both into a hug."

"I'm going to go and ask Varis—" Rolen started.

"What is going on out here now?" Mr. R clipped in Varis' dry voice. "Why does it smell like burning flesh?"

"Ah, Varis," Rolen rolled his eyes. "We need you three to move. We'll set you up in the mansion. But it's no longer safe for use to be out here."

"What are you talking about?" Varis glared.

"We lost a friend to the evil force we're hunting," Rolen explained. "So unless you would like to join him on the astral plane, I suggest you get moving!"

"Varis nods and move to his tents. You hear him rustle the halflings and watch the three of them move their belongings inside the arcane door on the side of the wagon." Mr. R narrated.

"Once everyone goes inside, I'd like to pull Ront to the side," Torinn asked.

"What is it?" Ront asked.

"Are you sure about this?" Torinn questioned. "About giving your soul to the Raven Queen so a measly fey creature could pass on to the astral plane?"

"I'm sure," Ront assured him. "What's the point of endless servitude to the goddess of death, if not to help others in the final moments?"

"I just can't imagine eternity as Saint Peter to goddess of death," Torinn explained.

"It's nothing to worry about, my friend," Ront chuckled. "For one day you will meet me at the gates I guard. Two old friends uniting once more at the end of the road."

"As you both come to terms with what is to come," Mr. R began. "You both notice symbols in the palms of your hands. Ront, in your right palm, the sun symbol of Pelor shines brightly for a moment before fading into a scar. Torinn, your palm resembles the marking of the Raven Queen. Dark and black, fading into the shiny gold of your skin."

Ront and Torinn frowned to each other. Fighting back emotions. The stood from their chairs and buried themselves in a hug.

"You are my brother," Torinn began. "And I shall fight by your side until the very end."

"And I will fight with you until my dying breaths are drawn from my body."

I could feel my own tears begin to trickle down my cheek as I sniffed to clear my nose.

"You all make your ways to your rooms for the evening's rest," Mr. R broke in. Fighting through the knot in his throat. "Regaining any spell slots or lost hit points for the start of the next day."

IN PLAIN SIGHT

"You all awake the next morning," Mr. R continued. "There's an eerie feeling you all have. Pre-apocalypse jitters we'll call it. That feeling of walking into something you know is not going to be easy and will definitely have consequences. When you make your way into the dining room for the breakfast spread, you all are met by Varis and the twins."

"You're all up early." I yawned. "I sit down and start my breakfast routine."

"Elves don't sleep," Rolen reminded me.

"They're still early," I mumbled, shoving the last three bites of pizza into my mouth.

"Ugh," Rolen groaned. "Do you ever not eat?"

"Nope!" I smiled.

"So now that you all have rested, would someone mind explaining the events of the previous evening?" Varis broke through. "Why were we cremating a boggle? Where did you even come across one of those creatures?"

"What do you mean?" Lerissa asked.

"What do I mean?" Varis raised his eyebrow. "Boggles are not native to this area. They don't come from this plane either. Boggles reside at the rift between us and the feywild," he explained. "And usually are just there to trick and play with travelers. So again I ask, why were you cremating a boggle all the way out here?"

"He showed up here last night in my room," Lerissa began explaining. "Trying to kidnap me and take me to Faria."

"And why Faria?" Varis continued to question.

"The evil dark entity guy thing that we're trying to destroy is there," Ront answered.

"He sent Oggie—"

"What's an Oggie?" Varis interrupted Lerissa.

"The boggle," Lerissa groaned. "He was sent here to retrieve me. For some reason this damn necromancer, wannabe lich, god-like freak has an obsession with the powers I possess. He has also held captive another powerful wizard prodigy for months now. And we're still unsure about why."

"So what do you think he wants?" Arila's voice cut in.

"I'm not quite sure. All I know is he needs a lot of arcane power to do whatever he's attempting." Lerissa sighed. "Last time we faced off against him, he was in the beginning stages of the family blood ritual of becoming a lich. We managed to stop him then, but he escaped and we've been on the chase ever since."

"So this new empire that's been rising in the world, quickly conquering and slaughtering whole civilizations, this is his doing as well?" Elton now asked.

"Yes," Torinn joined. "He's amassed an army ten times the

size it once was. Kidnapping the young, training prisoners as meat shields, and worst of all, raising the dead."

"And how do you know that?" Varis asked.

"We've been fighting his armies in every city and kingdom we waltz into. Liberating them from this tyranny. But after we liberate them, a swarm of undead flock the town, nearly destroying them," Rolen explained.

"So to stop this mass extinction of the world, you must destroy the ultimate power." Arila pieced together.

"Bingo," Ront said. "Once he falls, his army has no leader. The undead soldiers fall without a power to keep them 'alive'."

"But what if they're more of a hydra instead of a colony of illithids?" Elton scoffed.

"Because he acts more as a single leader, or elder brain," Lerissa described. "Giving actions to his armies for his own benefit. He has no subordinates that would take power from him. He knows what kind of leadership that breeds."

"This is a being who's trying to 'live' forever." Ront shook his head. "He wouldn't risk being betrayed by anyone. To lose his power to a companion. This is his army. And he wants everyone to know it."

"So what's the plan then?" Varis wondered.

"It doesn't matter." Rolen raised his eyebrow. "You three are heading the opposite direction."

"But you've had to have thought of something," Varis said.

"We have." Rolen eyed Mr. R.

"You can share with us," Arila joined. "We're not going to tell them."

"Why do you want to know so much?" Ront asked.

"Because strategy is a good thing to discuss," Elton explained. "So tell us. How do you plan on defeating Greg?"

"I throw my dagger at Elton!" Ront shouted out. "Twenty-three!"

"You chuck your dagger," Mr. R began. "Regular dagger or Raven dagger?"

"Poisoned," Ront answered.

"What would you do that for?" Torinn asked.

"Just wait," Ront said.

"You throw this dagger and it lands in Elton's right shoulder. Roll me damage."

"Is there sneak attack damage?" Liam questioned.

"I'll say yes since this was a random attack," Mr. R answered.

"Forty points of piercing damage." Liam rolled. "And six poison damage."

"As the dagger protrudes out of the halfling's shoulder," Mr. R narrated. "For a moment nothing happens. But as the poison begins to settle, you watch as Elton no longer is Elton. His body morphs and shifts into a tall, blackish-blue, mouthless, alien looking creature. It lets out a grunt of pain as it stares at the dagger in its shoulder. Everyone roll initiative."

We all rolled our dice.

"Ten," Jacob began.

"Thirteen!" Ben followed.

"Ten," Laura echoed Jacob.

"Twenty-three." Liam smirked.

"Eleven," Daryl shrugged.

Everyone turned to look at me. My eyes were wide. I held up my index finger and hung my head. "It's at least a three when I add my modifier." I cringe-smiled.

"Well at least our two who do most damage are spread out," Torinn noted. "Maybe then we'll all get a hit on these guys!"

"Ront, you start. What do you follow up with?" Mr. R asked.

"Oh really?" Liam asked. "They don't get a reaction to my first attack—" He jolted in his seat. He turned his head and glared at Ben, who was giving him that shut-up death stare.

"No," Mr. R answered. "Because it was considered a sneak attack, they don't."

"Wonderful." Ront smiled. He clapped his hands together and rubbed them back and forth. "I'm going dash across the room at fake Elton."

Mr. R clicked around on his laptop until sliding a window across to the table screen. On it was a battle map of the dining hall. He took our miniatures from the corner of the table and roughly placed them on the map. Individually we all moved them into the position we wanted to be in. Mr. R then turned around to the shelf of minis behind him and pulled down five figures.

"Alright." Mr. R nodded to Ront. "You dash, five, ten, fifteen, twenty feet." He counted out as he moved the half-orc mini each square. "Leaving you still with ten feet of movement."

"Okay." Liam bit his lip. "I'm right on top of it now correct?"

Mr. R nodded again.

"Then with my action, I take out the Raven dagger and jam it into one of its eyes." Liam narrated. He picked up his d20 again and gave it a roll. "Twelve?"

"Doesn't hit," Mr. R answered. "You run at the creature in a blur, stopping at the end of the table just short of the creature. In a downward swing, you just miss the creature's face."

"Crap!" Liam cursed under his breath. "Can I use my left-over movement to get away?"

Mr. R shook his head. "You used your movement action and your attack action. You're out of actions."

"I guess that's it," Liam sighed.

"As you charge at the creature and miss your attack," Mr. R rolled, "the beast reaches out to slam you but misses as you miss your swing. It tries to grab you again." He rolled a second time. "This time it slams its fists into your side. You take seven bludgeoning damage—"

"I use Uncanny Dodge," Liam interrupted.

"Roll me a dex save then," Mr. R asked.

"Twenty-two."

"In your reaction, you manage to duck as the monster's fists swing just over your head." Mr. R narrated. "As that is happening, Adrik, Varis is going to attack you. Sixteen hit?"

I rolled my eyes and nodded.

"You take seven damage as Varis slams you in the chest, knocking you out of your seat and onto the floor," Mr. R continued.

"Can I use my reaction attack?" I asked.

"You are prone. It would take the action to stand. And the reaction is only for attacks—"

"I do it from the ground then," I interjected.

"Alright, how do you do this?" Mr. R asked with a smile.

"As he knocks me back, I would like to pull one of my handaxes from my belt and give it a nice hurl at his face." I returned the smile. I rolled my d20 into the middle of the table. It landed on eight just before knocking over my figure. "Plus nine making that a seventeen."

"Hits. Roll me some damage." Mr. R nodded.

I searched my dice bag trying to find my d6 when Mr. R spoke up again.

"Hold on." He searched his notes. "That attack roll needs to be with disadvantage."

"What?" I blurted out. "Why?"

"You're still attuned to that berserker axe, correct?" Mr. R raised his eyebrow.

"Yeah." I eyed him.

"Read the card for that weapon," Mr. R said.

I shuffled through my binder for the laminated piece of paper labeled *Berserker Axe*. "When attuned you are unwilling to put the axe down and have disadvantage with any other weapon—" I read aloud. Without arguing, I picked my d20 back up and rolled again. "Well that's good, I rolled a twenty-six on my second roll. So seventeen still hits."

"As you hit the hard ground with a thud," Mr. R narrated, "You instinctively pull an axe from your belt. Giving it a nice throw, it finds its mark and splits open Varis' forehead. What's the damage?"

"Seven slashing damage," I answered.

"As the axe sends Varis back a couple steps, he catches his balance and moves back at you again. Raising his hands high above his head, he slams into you on the ground." Mr. R rolled. "And misses as you roll to the left." He looked at his map. He eyed the minis for a moment before looking back at his notes. "As that happens, Gimble, Arila moves to attack you." He rolled again. "Twenty-five is going to—"

"I use Cutting Words!" Jacob shouted. But he stopped. Thought for a second. "Never mind. I don't do that yet. Continue."

"It's going to hit," Mr. R finished his sentence. "Dealing seven—"

"Cutting Words!" Jacob interrupted again. "I rolled a nine!"

Mr. R took a deep breath and laughed. "Alright."

"As she winds up to hit me, I sing, *hit me, baby, one more time!*" Jacob continued.

"Arila winds her hands up and moves to swing at you." Mr. R began. "But as your words escape your mouth she's caught off guard by you singing to her about wanting to be hit. When her arms come full swing into your chest, she merely taps you, bumping you back a step."

"Perfect!" Jacob leaned back and folded his arms.

"But she's going to hit you, *baby, one more time.*" Mr. R smiled.

"Crap," Jacob slumped forwards again.

"Thirteen, that meets your armor class," Mr. R mumbled to himself. "Meaning you take seven points of bludgeoning damage."

"Ouch," Gimble grunted.

"Can't you dodge like Ront?" I asked.

"Not for three more levels. And that's if I continue pursuing rogue as a class," Jacob explained.

"As Arila shakes her head and focuses again, she swings her hands back around in a circle and slams your chest. Knocking you back a couple steps." Mr. R narrated. He turned to Ben, "You're up."

"I cast Entangle on fake Varis," Ben directed.

"Okay," Mr. R nodded. "Adrik, I'll need a strength saving throw from you."

"Seventeen?" I winced at Ben.

He shook his head. "My bad." He closed his eyes and frowned. "We'll take him out and drop the spell before he can attack."

"You'd better," I scowled.

Mr. R pointed at Daryl while still writing behind his screen.

"I move at Varis and attack him with my mace," Daryl explained. "Sixteen?"

"Hits," Mr. R answered.

"I deal twelve bludgeoning damage." Daryl rolled.

"Charging at the now entangled Varis, you underarm swing your mace, connecting with Varis' chin. With a loud crack, you watch as his jaw dangles for a moment before his entire form begins to shift into that of the previous monster that took Elton's form," Mr. R narrated. "Its glowing yellow eyes locking onto yours."

"I squint right back," Torinn said.

Mr. R pointed his pencil back over to Jake. "Your turn."

"Alright," Gimble cheered. "I'll start off by apologizing to my sweet Arila. Then I stab her with my rapier," he sighed. "Eight. I'm guessing that doesn't hit?"

Mr. R shook his head.

"Well, crap." Gimble frowned.

"As you lunge at her with your rapier, the thin blade pokes her leather chest piece, arching your rapier as if you were merely fencing with her." Mr. R chuckled. "Lerissa, your move."

Laura pursed her lips in thought, rolling her d20 between her palms. "I'm going to cast Magic Missile at third level." She marked her spell in her binder. "I'm going to blast two missiles at each of these... doppelgangers?"

"Alright, roll me six attacks," Mr. R said.

"Twenty-two, thirteen, nat twenty which makes that thirty, another nat twenty! Twelve and..." she rolled her sixth roll. "Nineteen."

"Let's see." Mr. R finished writing. "Hit, miss, crit, crit, miss, and hit."

"Okay, so the first hit I want on Arila. I'll miss fake Elton. Crit on fake Varis. Comes back around to crit on Arila, miss again on Elton, and final blast on Varis," Lerissa directed.

"Give me individual damage per being hit," Mr. R asked.

"Alright, Arila takes—" Laura rolled. "Seven fire damage. And Varis takes—" She rolled again. "Twelve fire damage."

Mr. R scribbled down the damage in his notes and looked back up. "Lerissa, watching your friends miss their attacks and entangle each other, you slam your staff into the ground and blast six bolts of fire in the three different directions—"

"Wait!" Laura blurted out. "If Varis is grappled don't I get advantage?"

"Yes," Mr. R answered. "However, with how you chose your attacks to hit, it wouldn't affect the two that missed Elton."

Laura frowned. "You're right," she sighed.

"These six arcane blasts shoot out from the top of your staff," Mr. R continued narrating. "Four of them finding their marks. First stunning the doppelganger, then full blasting the two. Destroying Arila's form and reverting to the same dark figure as the other two." Mr. R sipped his drink. "The other two arcane blasts struggle to target the final doppelganger and singe the wooden table." He jotted a few more notes, then pointed his pencil at me. "To start your turn, I need a strength saving throw."

I shook my d20 in my fist and gave it a toss. "Twenty-five." I smirked, folding my arms.

"As the doppelganger in front of you is blasted with an arcane energy, you tug and pull on the vines that were created to hold you both in place," Mr. R depicted. "Gaining some wiggle room before managing to tear free of the arcane vines."

"Perfect," I snarled. "I go into a frenzied rage! Using one of my actions to stand. Followed by two swift attacks with my axe." I rolled again. "Twenty-two and twenty-eight." I didn't wait for him to tell me if they hit. I know they hit. "First hit deals thirteen slashing damage. Second one deals seventeen slashing damage."

"Explain his death for me," Mr. R asked.

"Ha-ha!" I cheered. "As I rise to my feet, dusting off the vines on my shoulders. I reach behind me and grab my axe off my back. I give it a single twirl before gripping it with both hands. In an upward swing I thrash through his front, and with the returning momentum, I drop the axe down, splitting his head! And as I'm bathed in doppelganger blood, I let out a booming laugh. Ah-ha-ha-ha!"

Mr. R reached over and set the figure in front of me on its side. "And that circles us back to the top of the round. Ront?" He pointed.

"If I used dash as my bonus action and moved behind him, can I use sneak attack?" Liam asked.

Mr. R contemplated for a moment. "Give me a stealth check. If it succeeds then I'll allow it."

"Well, my stealth is a plus seventeen," Liam noted. "It's most likely going to succeed."

Mr. R nodded. "You're right. I'll allow the sneak attack then."

"Awesome. Then I use my dash bonus action to get behind and plunge my dagger into its back," Liam narrated. "Twenty-four hits. So that'll deal... thirty-nine points of piercing damage. Also dealing three points of necrotic damage."

"As you dart behind the doppelganger, drawing your blade and piercing it into the blackish skin, the monster lets out a groan of pain. It turns towards you and glares," Mr. R narrated. "And then its form begins to shift. Its skin turning green, bottom jaw protruding, large teeth growing from inside its new mouth. After only a moment, you stand staring at yourself."

Ront groaned. "Not this cheesy crap—"

"Gimble, the doppelganger nearest you winds up to slam you," Mr. R rolled. "Hitting with a twenty. As your body checks backward, taking seven damage, it winds up to do it again."

"Cutting Words!" Gimble blurted out again.

"And that causes the second attack to miss." Mr. R chuckled. "As the doppelganger swings its arms at you, you duck, sending the monster into a slight spin. Making it Rolen's turn."

"I drop my Entangle spell, letting the dead doppelganger fall to the ground, and I move around the entire table towards Ront and his doppelganger," Rolen explained.

"Okay," Mr. R acknowledged. "That moves it to Torinn."

"I want to follow Rolen and attack the doppelganger," Torinn explained.

"Which one do you attack?" Mr. R asked.

"What'd you mean?" Torinn raised his eyebrow.

"There are two Ronts staring at each other. Which one would you like to attack?" Mr. R asked again.

"Not this crap!" Torinn sighed.

"That's what I said!" Ront blurted out.

"Can I percept which is which?" Daryl questioned.

"You can sure try," Mr. R answered.

Daryl pulled up his dice case and sorted through it for a moment, picking up one die, then dropping it and picking up another from a different part of the case. He sorted through them for a good moment or two before pulling out a really gross looking brown d20. He shook it in his fist for a moment before mumbling, "This one." He tossed it on the table. It rolled in a straight line before bouncing off the side of his glass he had on the table. When it finally stopped, it was hidden under the cover of his open binder. "Fifteen," he called out.

"They seem pretty identical. Not much to tell them apart," Mr. R began. "However, you notice a small wound in the shoulder blade of the Ront not facing you."

"That's the one I swing at!" Daryl blurted. "Seventeen?"

"Hits," Mr. R nodded.

"I deal six bludgeoning damage," Daryl frowned.

"How do you kill this doppelganger?" Mr. R asked.

"Yes!" Torinn cheered. "Like a bat, I throw my mace over my shoulder and give it a nice swing at its head. Smashing it into nothing but soup."

"In a shower of black liquid and chunks of pink meat, the second doppelganger falls to its knees, headless," Mr. R narrated. He turned to Gimble who was waiting with a smile.

"I cast Thunderwave at fourth level, to the theme of Thunderstruck!" Gimble said. "That'll be a constitution saving throw please."

Mr. R rolled. "Does not save."

"Wunderbar!" Gimble laughed. "That pushes the imposter of my sweet Arila ten feet back, and they take... twenty points of thunder damage."

"A shockwave of energy blasts out of your violin as you pull your bow across the strings," Mr. R began. "The blast throws the doppelganger back ten feet—" He moved the figure back two squares and tipped the other doppelganger over to signify its death. "Throwing plates and shattering glasses across the room, the doppelganger manages to stay on their feet and glares at you in anger."

"What can I say?" Gimble laughed. "I've got a soft spot for the gnomish ladies."

"Lerissa, that makes it your turn," Mr. R said.

"I cast Firebolt at the remaining doppelganger," Lerissa called out. "Sixteen hits, dealing fifteen fire damage."

"As the last doppelganger begins moving back towards Gimble, it's met with a bolt of fire in its chest, sending it back a few steps," Mr. R narrated. "Burning away some of the black skin and revealing a pink muscle underneath, the beast lets out a growl of pain from the blast." Mr. R pointed back at me. "Your turn."

"I'm gonna get over the table towards the doppelganger and swing my axe through its neck when I land." I smiled. "Twenty-three hits!" I rolled again. "Sixteen damage."

"How do you kill your second doppelganger?" Mr. R asked.

Everyone leaped from their chairs and cheered.

"Oh thank God!" Ront groaned.

"In the most fluid motion you've ever seen," I started. "I slide across the table. As I come to the end of the table I start my swing. Once I hit the ground, I've finished my swing and severed the head off the doppelganger. Once I finish, I reach over to the half-broken mug of ale on the table, take a sip, and say heads up!"

"Just for fun," Mr. R laughed. "Give me a performance check."

I bit my lip. "Twelve."

"You manage to slide, behead, and land. Even pick up the ale. But you mess up saying heads up." Mr. R smiled.

"Up heads!" I shouted. I grabbed my root beer and sipped it as if nothing happened.

"Standing inside your mansion now," Mr. R continued. "Amidst the black blood and bits of doppelganger brains everywhere, a deep, ominous chuckle breaks your momentary silence." Mr. R clicked his keyboard. The screen went dim. "You fools still believe you could beat someone as powerful as me?" A voice echoed. "You still believe there is hope for you?"

"We're not afraid of you anymore, Greg!" Rolen shouted.

"Greg is no more!" The voice boomed. "I have grown stronger than my mortal form! I have excelled past the teachings of the Raven Queen, the secrets of Vecna, and the power of Tiamat! I have become more powerful than the gods themselves! And I shall rule them all! The planes will finally bow to me - Asmodeus!"

Mr. R clicked his keyboard again and the screen grew bright again.

"And like that," Mr. R said. "The room is back to normal, except for one thing. The doppelganger bodies are no longer on the floor. Instead, they are replaced by those who they once personified. Laying on the floor are the deceased bodies of Varis, Elton, and Arila."

SACRIFICES

"We need to go!" Ront demanded.

"What about those three?" I asked.

"Forget them," Rolen shouted. "They're dead! We need to move!"

"Gather what you need," Lerissa directed everyone. "We need to close the mansion and get moving!"

"Can I loot their bodies?" I asked Mr. R.

"Why would you do that?" Torinn glared at me.

"Maybe they have something worth taking with us." I shrugged.

"Give me an investigation check," Mr. R said.

"Dude!" Ront shouted. "We need to go!"

I ignored him and rolled. "Seventeen."

"Looting through the three bodies, you find about thirty gold pieces, a couple daggers, and a potion of healing," Mr. R listed.

"Boom!" I threw my hands up. "Told you there would be something!"

"Great." Ront rolled his eyes. "Can we go then?"

"Well let's go!" I moaned. "I say while I'm already halfway out the door."

"You all gather and collect your things from the mansion," Mr. R narrated. "Once you're all collected, you assemble in the foyer."

"Do we still have access to a Teleport spell?" Rolen asked the group.

"I've still got my seventh level spell slot," Gimble answered.

"Don't use it!" Lerissa blurted out.

"Why?" Rolen eyed her. "We've got to hurry, don't we?"

"But what if we need to get out of there quickly?" Lerissa questioned. "What if he's too strong for us?"

"He's going to be too strong anyways!" Rolen reminded us. "I don't think this battle will be something we all walk away from."

"We said that last time," Lerissa recalled. "And look where we are now."

"Still chasing him around the world," Torinn joined in.

"We can defeat him," Lerissa assured them. "We've done it before."

"No we didn't." Rolen groaned. "He escaped. He's still at large."

"But we stopped him from completing his ritual," Lerissa continued to argue.

"We just delayed the ritual." Torinn sighed. "We didn't truly stop him. If anything, all we did was kill our only companion who could help us." Torinn glared at Ront.

"What's that look for?" Ront threw his hands up. "I was doing what he asked. He said it would work."

"But it didn't!" Torinn continued. "We're still chasing him around the world, and we're not really chasing him to chase him. We're chasing him because he still has Elfi. And someone has an obsession with the woman he's met once in his life."

"Don't drag me into this," Rolen defended. "I didn't ask for her to disappear. She needs our help as much as we need hers."

"We don't even know if he really has her," Ront argued. "All we've got are the claims of a bunch of his minions and an owlbear."

"We saw her last time," Rolen fought. "She was there."

"And how do we know he didn't kill her?" Torinn asked.

"Because if he did, he would've attempted at taking Lerissa by now!" Rolen shouted.

"He already did!" Ront clipped.

The room fell silent. Nobody moved. We hardly breathed. But the silence was quickly diminished by Lerissa sighing.

"He didn't." She broke in. "Oggie wasn't here for me. And I don't think the doppelgangers were either. They were here for this. I pull out the spell scroll from my lockbox."

"What is it?" I asked.

"It was the only thing my mother had left me before she left me on this plane," Lerissa explained. "It was her way of defending me."

"What's it do?" Gimble questioned.

"It's a scroll imbued with the arcane power to kill a being with one word," Lerissa choked out. "Sh-she left it for me in case I ever needed to escape a situation that was inescapable. She feared that I might fall victim to the tiefling slavers when she left me. This was to ensure that didn't happen."

"So why haven't we thought about using this on Greg?" Rolen eyed her.

"Because I'm still unsure whether it might actually be able to kill him." Lerissa began to tear up. "This spell could save us all one day. But only if it works!"

"What do you mean, if it works?" Ront asked.

"I mean, we still have to fight him." Lerissa began to cry. "We have to weaken him quite a bit before the spell can work."

"That's the easy part," I joined.

"The first step is to get there though," Gimble reminded everyone.

"Should we teleport?" Rolen asked. "If we need it, I guess I can Planeshift us out of there."

"How would we get back?" Torinn questioned.

"Let's cross that bridge when we get there," Gimble said. "For now, we need to move. We need to finish what we started."

"Then we teleport," Lerissa agreed. "We teleport into Faria. No ambush. He knows we're coming. That saves us a second teleport out."

"We're just going at this head on?" Torinn continued to ask.

"It wouldn't be us if we didn't," I quipped.

"That's suicide!" Torinn blasted.

"Maybe," Ront sighed. "But to save the world, we must make the sacrifice. If I recall a certain dragonborn I know once said that this is the price we pay in the line of work we do. We make sacrifices for the greater good. Now if I recall, he was telling us about a similar suicide mission."

"That was different," Torinn frowned.

"How?" Ront tilted his head. "We were chasing him down, saving innocent lives. He even attacked us."

Torinn pursed his lips. He knew Ront was right. He just wouldn't admit it. "Fine," Torinn sighed. "May Pelor have mercy on us all."

"And may the Raven Queen, too." Ront smiled. "Let's get out of here, then."

"As a group, you all climb down from the mansion entrance on the side of the wagon. As the last member climbs down, the arcane door vanishes from the side of the wagon," Mr. R narrated. "The world is silent. Eerily silent. As if everything in nature is aware of what's about to happen."

"Do I sense anything?" Rolen asked.

"Give me a perception check," Mr. R requested.

"Twenty?" Ben rolled.

"In the stillness of the world, you sense a slight disruption in nature. And from what you can feel, the disruption is growing, and growing, and growing," Mr. R intensified. "Like a large mass of nature is moving—migrating—in your direction."

"What do you mean?" Rolen raised his eyebrows.

"As you try to understand that feeling, you hear a rumbling out in the distance. Followed by the sounds of croaking frogs." Mr. R clicked his keyboard and the sounds faintly rang throughout the room.

"Guys, get together!" Rolen demanded.

"What is it?" I asked.

"I don't know. But it's moving fast," Rolen explained. "Somebody get us out of here!"

"As you all circle up and prepare for the feeling of teleporting," Mr. R sipped his drink. "A huge mass of frogs crests the horizon. The ground shaking at the masses of bullywugs and grungs charging and hopping in your direction."

"What are they doing?" Rolen asked.

"Roll me a history check," Mr. R said.

Ben eyed him again and rolled. "Seventeen?"

"You recall in your studies and time connecting with nature, the migration patterns of these creatures." Mr. R explained. "You remember a tale of a lake in the northern township of Faria. Lake Froggermoth. In bullywug culture, this is the site from which they emerged from mere frogs into humanoid beings. It is believed that the mighty froggermoth of the lake brought these beings to fruition. Guiding their ancestors from the feywild into the material plane. And every year about this time, the world's population of bullywugs, grungs, and even some fire newts and small groups of slaads migrate to this holy site to bring gifts and offerings to the great froggermoth."

"Should we still panic?" Torinn asked.

"No, just stay close," Rolen directed. "Get ready to teleport."

Mr. R slowly increased the sounds or frog croaking and feet stamping. We all reached out and held each other's hands until the sounds began to die down. Then, Gimble looked up and burst into song.

"Take us away, a better place, take us away!"

"And with the magic words of Natasha Bedingfield, you all feel the familiar rush of teleportation throwing you across the plane," Mr. R began narrating. "As the rush of air stops and you all feel like you've been shoved, you begin to notice the state of the town of Faria." He clicked his keyboard and the image changed. "The once-thriving town you recall from not that long ago looks barren and empty. No sign of life anywhere. The buildings look run down and looted. Some with wood planks in the window. Some reduced to rubble. In the distance, you can see some buildings that are burning. One, in particular, catches your eye. A tall building is burning from the bottom floor, as a family screams from the second story window."

"I run off towards that house!" Rolen shouted.

"No! Wait—" Ront tried to call out.

"Once I get close enough I cast Create Water. I want to make it rain over the building and put out the flames," Rolen continued over Ront's cries.

"Son of—" Ront growled under his breath. "I follow behind him."

"Rolen, what's your spell DC?" Mr. R asked.

"Nineteen," Ben answered.

"You channel the arcane energy of the nature around you. Focusing every particle of water in the area over this blazing fire." Mr. R narrated. "Just over the house, a cloud opens up, pouring rain down atop the house. The flames sputter and spit as the water snuffs out the fire. The family fearing for their lives, still trapped in the upstairs."

"I run inside," Liam directed.

"You run in to see the weakened structure of the building," Mr. R depicted. "Black and smoldering."

"Stairs?" Ront asked.

"A pile of ash under the access hole in the ceiling to the next floor," Mr. R explained.

Ront thought for a moment. "I'm going to climb up!"

"Give me an acrobatics check," Mr. R asked.

Liam rolled. "Thirteen." He winced.

"It's tough," Mr. R began. "The walls are still hot and crumbling with any contact. But you manage to get yourself up onto the floor of the next level. There, a family stands in fear as this half-orc in dark robes climbs up through the floor."

"Don't panic." Ront put his hands up to calm the family. "I'm here to help you—"

"As you say that, the foundation shifts, causing the floor you stand on to angle," Mr. R interrupted. "The furniture begins to move to the other side of the room."

"Is it going to harm them?" Ront asked.

"No, but the smashing of that dresser into the wall just might destroy this house," Mr. R explained.

"Crap!" Ront cursed under his breath.

"The dresser is moving fast!" Mr. R continued.

"I—uh." Ront scrunched his face. "I hurl my body at the dresser. Can I send it out a window or through the opposite wall? Make an easier escape?"

"You can sure try." Mr. R shrugged. He scanned through his notes for a second. "Let's make it an athletics check. Since you're both running and shoving."

Liam leaned forward against the table and rolled his d20. He frowned at the roll. "Thirteen?"

"In the spur of the moment you leap at the dresser, slamming your shoulder into its side," Mr. R narrated. "The dresser shifts against the far wall, slamming against it, but it continues sliding downwards with the angled floor."

"I get in front of it and try to slow it down," Ront continued strategizing.

"Give me a strength-saving throw," Mr. R asked.

Liam winced. "Five."

"You move in front of the sliding dresser and try to dig your heels into the floor to slow it down. But it's just—too—heavy!" Mr. R grunted. "As the dresser slams and pins you between it and the wall, you feel the foundation of the building fall again. The family panics."

"Can—I—" Ront struggled, "Can I reach my—dagger?"

"Give me a..." Mr. R clicked his tongue. "Give me a constitution save."

"Twenty-two." Liam rolled.

"You manage to move your free arm to your hip and pull out your dagger," Mr. R described. "The Raven Dagger I presume?"

Ront nodded. "I throw it so that I'm beside the family."

"That's a dexterity check," Mr. R said.

"Twenty-one," Ront answered.

"You throw the dagger across the room. Slamming it into the wall beside the panicking family, who are now freaking out even more." Mr. R continued to narrate. "In a flash of shadow, you bamf from behind the dresser to the other end of the room. Are you holding the dagger?"

"Yes!" Ront answered. "I pull the dagger from the wall and toss it into whatever window there is."

"Dexterity again."

"Twenty," Liam rolled.

"You pull the dagger, sliding along the angled floor again. You huck it at the open window frame and with another bamf, you teleport into the window," Mr. R depicted.

"I shout out the window, Rolen!" Liam cupped his mouth. "I've got the family in here safe—"

"As you say that, the building shifts again," Mr. R interrupted.

"I need your help!" Ront continued. "I'm going to start tossing them out the window! I need you to catch them!"

"What? No! I'm not the best option for that!" Rolen argued.

"Well at the moment, you're my only option!" Ront rebutted. "I turn back inside and tell the family to one by one slide to me."

Mr. R rolled a couple of times. "They seem a little hesitant."

"Trust me!" Ront shouted.

"Give me a persuasion check," Mr. R asked.

"Seventeen," Liam clipped.

"They hesitate again, but slowly they move their smallest child, a young boy, towards the wall," Mr. R narrated. "The boy holds his mother's hand as she positions him to slide to you. She closes her eyes as she lets him go. Make a dexterity check."

"Seventeen again!" Liam blurted.

"The little boy slides along the floor at you," Mr. R began. "You snag him by the arm and swing him up into the window with you."

"Rolen!" Ront shouted again. "Are you ready?"

"No!" Rolen replied.

"Catch!"

"Ront, give me a strength check. Rolen make me a dexterity saving throw," Mr. R asked.

"Twenty!" Liam said.

"I cast Enhance Ability!" Ben blurted out. "I use it on my dexterity. I get advantage on all dex checks!"

Mr. R nodded.

"Good, because that's a three on my first roll," Rolen groaned. And then he almost burst out into hysterical laughter! "And that's a two!"

"Can I use a reaction?" Ront asked.

"What is your reaction?" Mr. R questioned.

"I leap after the kid after I throw him," Ront explained.

"Give me another dexterity saving throw," Mr. R said.

"Fifteen!" Liam rolled.

"You leap from the window, just managing to snag the child," Mr. R narrated. "And in the instant of tucking the child into your chest and preparing to take the fall, a presence comes over you. One you recognize. A cold presence that wraps around you." Mr. R paused. "And then you hit the ground. But something in between you and the hard ground. As you get up with the child, you feel something on your back that wasn't there a moment ago. Rolen, before you stands Ront. Behind him, large, black wings protruding from his back."

"No—way!" Rolen's jaw dropped.

"I did it," Ront mumbled. "Can I move them?"

"It takes a second, but the wings begin to move at your command," Mr. R explained.

"I blast off the ground and fly back up to the house." Ront directed.

"One by one, you help the last three family members down from the top floor. Carefully floating them down to Rolen," Mr. R narrated.

"Is that all of them?" Rolen asked.

"That's all of them," Ront answered.

"Once they're collected together," Rolen sighed, "I Wild Shape myself into a giant eagle."

"I'm guessing we're going to fly off and gather with the party?" Ront asked.

Rolen nodded and gave a coo.

"We take off to find the rest of the group then," Ront directed.

"You both spread your wings and blast off into the sky," Mr. R narrated. "Looking down upon the decimated town of Faria."

FEARS AND NIGHTMARES

"ADRIK, TORINN, LERISSA, AND GIMBLE," MR. R continued. "You watch as Ront and Rolen take off towards the screams for help coming from deep within the city. But before you can react, your path is blocked." He clicked his keyboard.

On the screen, in front of the destroyed city, appeared six zombies, one being an ogre zombie, all led by what looked like a wight.

"Hobbling up the road towards you four, they move into flanking position. Circling you all." Mr. R narrated. "The wight unsheathes his longsword and drags it across the ground." He cleared his throat. "You are not to disturb the master," Mr. R growled. "And with that, the wight is going to charge at you all. Roll me initiative."

"Seven," Daryl groaned.

"That's better than my three," Laura quipped.

"Eighteen," I announced.

"Twelve," Jacob finished.

"Alright," Mr. R said as he jotted down his notes. "Adrik you're first."

"Is the wight still charging us?" I asked.

Mr. R nodded. Still not looking up from his notes.

"Then I would like to frenzy rage!" I announced.

"Now I want to make a note," Mr. R looked up. "You have already frenzied and not had any rest between. So you will be double exhausted if you survive this combat."

"Oh," I sighed. "Then can I just rage?"

"Yes," Mr. R nodded. "But you still have disadvantage since you frenzied once already."

"You're right," I agreed. "Then I'll just normal rage, and charge the wight. I want to start with a mid-section slash followed by a hack at his back." I explained. I rolled my d20 four times. "Thirteen and nineteen on the first hit. Twenty-six and thirteen again on the second."

"Both attacks just miss," Mr. R said. "You take off towards the charging wight, full swing. Your axe slides off the leather armor, dealing no damage, while your backswing just doesn't land and ends up on the ground behind the wight." He jotted down more notes and rolled his dice. "In retaliation, the wight is going to attack back. Taking a spinning swing, and missing with an eight. He's going to take his second attack. Grabbing your arm, you feel the frigid cold of the wight's skin as it grabs you. But nothing happens. Making it Gimble's turn."

"Are the zombies and wight within fifteen feet of me?" Gimble asked.

Mr. R scratched his chin. He moved to his laptop and played around with it for a second. Then he threw up a makeshift battle map. On the screen, he created placement holders for all attackers and moved our figures onto the grid.

"Yeah, I'd say they'd be in that vicinity if you moved a little more center."

"Then I do that," Gimble nodded. "I move to the center and cast Thunderwave at first level."

"Your spell DC is seventeen, right?" Mr. R asked.

"Yes, sir-roonie!" Jacob sang.

"Alright, roll me damage," Mr. R asked.

"Eighteen," Gimble rolled.

Mr. R clicked and dragged the wight and the ogre two squares backward. Leaving the other five zombies still.

"The blast of energy explodes from the tiny gnome bard, sending the wight and ogre backward." Mr. R narrated. "Seemingly unaffected by the blast, the five zombies converge on you four. Ending each of their turns just feet away. Making it Torinn's turn."

"I cast Dispel Evil And Good!" Daryl readily answered. "I move over to the wight and dismiss him back to his home plane!"

"Alright," Mr. R nodded. He pulled out his handbook and sifted through the back section. "Your spell DC is seventeen also, correct?"

"Yes sir," Daryl replied.

"Okay," Mr. R rolled. "As the divine arcane energy begins to shimmer from your amulet, you watch as the wight begins to fade from existence. Where he was once holding onto Adrik's arm, he no longer exists, blinking out of this plane." Mr. R shrugged. "And with that, the five zombies and one ogre zombie crumple to their feet and lay upon the ground. Once again becoming the corpses they are."

"Man," Lerissa sighed. "I never get to have any fun!"

"Sorry," Torinn apologized. "I didn't think that would stop all of them."

"It's probably for the best. Saves us some spell slots and hit points." Gimble reminded them.

"Does anyone have the possibility to remove my exhaustion?" I asked.

"Here," Jacob answered. "I cast Greater Restoration on him." He turned to me and busted into the Carlton in his chair. "Wake me up, before you go-go. Won't leave you hanging on like a yo-yo!" He sang.

"And with that tune," Mr. R began. "You feel alive and energized once again."

"Can Rolen and I find the party yet?" Ront interjected.

"Give me an investigation check," Mr. R replied.

"Twenty-two," Liam rolled.

"You both soar for a couple of moments before a glimmer catches your eye back where you left your group." Mr. R narrated. "You see Torinn on the ground, the group surrounded, and then the attackers just collapse."

"I shout at Rolen, they're down there! Let's go! And I dive towards them." Ront directed.

"Roll me a perception check both of you," Mr. R asked, pointing at Liam and Ben.

Liam eyed his uncle.

"Nine," Rolen winced.

"Twenty-seven," Ront frowned.

"Ront, a second glimmer catches your eye as a ball of flames is hurtling towards you both," Mr. R depicted. "You have one reaction."

Ront's eyes grew wide with options. "I-I—" He stuttered. "I slam into Rolen and knock him out of the way!"

"Rolen, as you move to dive towards your companions, you feel a heavy force slam you away from your target, sending you spinning off course and into the roof of a nearby building," Mr. R narrated. "Ront, you take—" He rolled a handful of dice. "Thirty..." He continued adding, "Thirty-six points of fire damage. And you are blasted out of the sky. Plummeting to the earth, you'll take—"

"I cast Mage Hand!" Gimble and Lerissa shouted simultaneously.

"Do you both cast it?" Mr. R asked.

They looked at each other and nodded.

"Alright," Mr. R continued. "Ront, as you're blasted out of the sky by a ball of fire, two arcane hands appear under you. Unable to hold your weight, they push up on you slowing down your descent to the earth." Mr. R rolled. "Taking half of sixteen falling damage."

"Well that's no good," Ront groaned as he deduced his damage.

"I told you," Mr. R boomed. His voice rang throughout the house. "They will perish at your hands!"

Mr. R clicked the keyboard and the zombies and wight disappeared. Replacing them was the image of a gnome, floating in the air. His left eye glowing an emerald green and misting off the side. A long black robe, tattered and worn, stretched just inches off the ground.

"You incompetent swine!" Greg growled.

"I drop Wildshape," Rolen grumbled. "Where is she!"

"Pathetic!" Greg continued to insult. "In the presence of the greatest being to ever live, and all you're worried about is your weakling of a companion."

"I said..." Rolen glared. "Where—is—she!" He shouted.

"And I use my last Wildshape and shift into an adult red dragon!"

"Alright," Mr. R nodded. "With that, I need you all to roll initiative once again."

"I swear, the next initiative roll might literally kill me!" Laura groaned. "Four." She folded her arms and sat back.

"I'm right there with you," Ben sighed. "Three."

"Well, I'm glad I don't have your luck," Jacob nudged Laura. "I rolled a twenty."

"I rolled an eleven," I joined.

"Nineteen," Liam followed.

"And I sit right in the middle with a seven." Daryl finished.

"Then let's get into this," Mr. R clapped his hands together and rubbed them. "Gimble, you get the first action."

Gimble drew in a deep breath. "I move over to Ront and cast Cure Wounds on him." He rolled his d8. "Giving him twelve hit points to his name." He marked off his used spell. "And then I want to inspire him," he shuffled through his binder. "Ront, my confidant. I don't mean to flaunt, but this is redonk."

We sat there, mouths gaping at what we just heard.

"What? It was off the top of my head." Gimble defended.

Mr. R cleared his throat. "Ront, take one d10 inspiration." Mr. R marked his notes. "And that then moves it to your turn, Ront."

Ront shook his head for a moment. "I move between everyone and Greg," He explained. "Spreading my wings to give them all cover from any of his attacks."

"Is that your entire turn?" Mr. R asked.

"To finish it," Ront swallowed. "I pull out the Raven dagger."

"Okay," Mr. R nodded. He began to chuckle that ominous chuckle he does before becoming Greg. "You think she will save you now? You surprise me with how naive you truly are." Greg scoffed. "And with that," Mr. R came back. "He throws both his arms out wide with a blast of lightning arcing into the buildings beside him. Blowing them off their foundations and revealing two large spires protruding out and arching over the ground. Hanging off the spires by their hands are Elfi on the left and the gnome child on the right."

Mr. R clicked his keyboard and the spires appeared on the image.

"Witness my children, true—raw—unlimited power. You six shall witness the coming of a new god!" Greg bellowed. "I—AM—ASMODEUS!" Mr. R cleared his throat. "And with a red blast of arcane energy blasting out from the pointed ends of the spires and screams of pain from the two hanging from said spires, Greg's body begins to shift. Growing from his forehead, large red horns curl upwards. His green eye fades from its emerald green to a shining crimson, ruby red." Mr. R clicked his keyboard again. The image of Greg faded into an image of a satanic-looking creature.

The horns curled upwards, the red eye, his legs changed into hairy goat hooves, and his black, tattered cloak became a red gown with spiked shoulders.

"Holy shit," Torinn mumbled.

"Now!" Asmodeus boomed. "Kneel before your new god!"

"I don't think so!" I laughed.

"Then you shall die!" Asmodeus threatened. "Adrik, that moves to your turn," Mr. R said.

"Hey, Ass-is-my-face!" I taunted. "I frenzy rage and charge at him with my axe!"

"Adrik, no!" Ront shouted at me. But I ignored him.

"Twenty-one, twenty-three, and twenty-nine!" I rolled.

"Are you using the berserker axe?" Mr. R asked.

I nodded.

"All three are a hit." Mr. R announced. "Roll me damage."

"Eleven, sixteen, and fifteen!" I called out. "Making it forty-two total."

"Adrik, in his barbarian rage, charges at Asmodeus with his axe held high. He smashes once into Asmodeus' chest. The second slash across the previous wound. And finally, a third slash burying itself into the wounds' intersection." Mr. R rolled his dice. "Adrik," He turned towards me, handing me a laminated piece of paper. "You feel a dark, evil, arcane energy flow through your arms, pulsing your muscles. You have reached the second level of attunement with the axe you carry."

I flipped the paper over.

Blood of the Damned

Chaotic-evil

Once attuned and cursed by the Berserker axe, when user attacks a being of undead, fey, or primordial being, the axe is imbued with the strengthening arcane powers of said being.

+5 on all attack and damage rolls while wielding the berserker axe.

Curse still applies.

I glared at Mr. R in fear.

He smiled back at me and whispered, "Adrik." Mr. R turned back to address everyone. "And with a blast of energy from the third attack, everyone make me a constitution saving throw."

We all looked at each other for a moment.

"Two," Jacob sighed.

"Three," Liam groaned.

"Fifteen," I joined.

"Seven!" Laura added to the moans.

"Nine," Daryl mumbled.

"Nat twenty," Ben laughed.

"What the hell?" Laura blurted out.

"What?" Ben looked at her confused.

"Why are you the only one who saved?" Daryl asked.

"Hey!" I argued. "I rolled a fifteen!"

"Everyone takes nine points of thunder damage. Adrik and Rolen take half." Mr. R distributed. "And everyone but those two are sent back ten feet."

"You're kidding!" Ront shouted.

Mr. R reached over to the mini figures on the table and moved the four set pieces back two squares. He looked up and pointed over to Daryl. "You're up."

"I want to channel my faith to Pelor, clutching my amulet, and casting Spiritual Weapon," Torinn narrated. "I create a javelin of arcane energy and throw it at Ass-modeus." He mocked. "Twenty-eight hits. It deals... thirteen force damage. And since it's move within five feet of him, as a bonus action I want to do it again. This time leaving the javelin inside his chest like a lightning rod." Daryl rolled again. "Twenty also hits, dealing... seventeen force damage."

"As your amulet begins to shine its familiar bright hue, a long spear of arcane light emerges from it," Mr. R depicted. "You pull it from the amulet and hurl it at Asmodeus. The arcane light piercing through his chest. It tears through his red robes and out his back. Flying through the air, it stops mid-air and reverses its course. Piercing another hole through Asmodeus' chest. The spear of light now protruding from his chest begins to attract the arcane electricity coming from the spires. You hear Elfi and the gnome child let out another cry of pain. He turned to Laura and pointed to her. "Your turn."

She glared at Mr. R for a moment. "How damaged does he look right now?"

"Give me a perception check," Mr. R asked.

"Seventeen," Laura squinted.

"He looks pretty damaged from what he's taken," Mr. R explained.

Laura took in a deep breath and pulled out a piece of paper from her binder. It was rolled into a scroll, sealed with wax, and wrapped in a red ribbon. "I open the scroll and cast Power Word Kill." She slowly opened the scroll and read it aloud. "Seferati, montoura ser'lahee. Quar insaya temouria tookoon." Her face shifted into sorrow.

"You all watch as Lerissa recites the spell from her scroll. When the last syllable leaves her mouth, the scroll bursts into flames in her hands." Mr. R narrated. "A gust of wind begins to kick up and swirl the dust around her. Lerissa's eyes flash white and bright as she's lifted off her feet and into the air. You hear Asmodeus screaming," Mr. R cleared his throat. "No! It can not be!" he cleared his throat again. "In a spectacle of arcana and nature, you all witness as Asmodeus begins to fade out of existence. Like a leaf blower to a sandcastle. Particle by particle being blasted away."

"It can't be that easy!" I mumbled.

"The wind begins to pick up and blast the sands and debris around you all." Mr. R continued.

"Can we still move?" Ben asked.

"Those who are strong enough, yes." Mr. R answered.

"I call out to Adrik," Rolen shouted. "Help me recover Elfi and the child!"

"I move towards the spires!" I directed.

"The sand and soil blasting you as you fight the spinning winds," Mr. R narrated. "The closer you get, arcs of electricity begin to catch you. Freezing your muscles for seconds at a time. But you endure. Taking—" He rolled. "Twenty points of damage total. Ten after your rage and resistance."

"I get Elfi first," I told him.

"You untie and pull Elfi from the spire."

"Get on Rolen's back!" I shouted at her. "And then I move to the kid."

"You fight through the elements, things kicking up and smacking you, and you hear a voice echo in your head." Mr. R leaned in. "Adrik!"

"Who's there?" I asked.

"Adrik!" Mr. R continued to whisper. "I'm your axe, Adrik. I crave blood. Feed me. Feed my hunger! And with that, you feel a sudden urge, not to save the child. But to kill him. Give me a wisdom saving throw!"

I rolled, and I don't think it could have been any worse! "Two," I sighed.

"Suddenly your rage and frenzy begin to cloud your mind," Mr. R narrated. "Your vision goes red as you stare at this helpless child. You charge towards them, axe held high over your head."

"How do I fight this?" I screamed.

"Do I notice this?" Ben asked.

"All you see is Adrik running towards the child you told him to set free," Mr. R answered.

"What about me?" Liam asked.

"Give me a perception check," Mr. R replied.

Liam rolled. His uncle rolled. They both looked up at each other.

"Twenty-four," Liam said.

"You notice Adrik charging at the spire with the still child still chained to it." Mr. R explained. "But you feel a tugging in your hand."

"My dagger?" Liam asked.

Mr. R nodded. "Your dagger is tugging your hand towards the charging Adrik."

"I take its lead!" Ront shouted.

"You lift off your feet and fly towards Adrik at top speed," Mr. R continued. "Your wings stop you in front of the charging barbarian."

"Why'd they stop?" Ront asked looking around at his back.

"Get out of the way!" I growled.

"Adrik," My axe whispered again. "He stands in our way! Kill him! Feed my thirst!"

"Ront! Move!" I shouted at him.

"I need you to roll an attack, Adrik," Mr. R said.

I shook my head and frowned. "Thirty-four."

"Uncanny Dodge!" Ront blurted out.

"Do I see this?" Daryl asked.

"Perception check," Mr. R pointed at Daryl. "Dexterity check," He moved his finger to Liam.

"Sixteen," Liam called out.

"Nat twenty!" Daryl cheered.

"Torinn," Mr. R began. "You turn your eyes just off the dissolving body of Asmodeus and watch as Adrik swings his axe down upon Ront. Ront, whom you see try to dive out of the way, just doesn't manage it. Adrik, can you give him his damage please?"

I rolled, fighting back angry tears. "Eighteen slashing damage."

"You take half that," Mr. R explained. "Adrik," that familiar whisper came through Mr. R's mouth. "Kill him! Give me strength!"

"I'm sorry," I choked out. "Thirty-one—"

"I run to Ront's aid!" Torinn interrupted.

"Alright," Mr. R nodded. "Give me an athletics check."

Daryl stared at Mr. R with wide eyes. Like he was speaking a foreign language.

"Give me an athletics check," Mr. R repeated himself.

Daryl shook his head, regaining his composure, and rolled. His face broke into another reaction of disbelief. We all lean in to see what he rolled.

"No f-ing way!" Liam laughed.

"You've got to be cheating!" Jacob joked.

"That's definitely a rare occurrence," Mr. R chuckled as he sat back down.

Torinn had rolled a second natural twenty. That's two in a row! Maybe this gross d20 was actually good luck.

"As Adrik hoists his axe over his head once again to attack Ront," Mr. R narrated. "The axe comes down and stops with what can only be described as—" He clicked his keyboard and a church bell rang through the house. "With a blast of light, you're all momentarily blinded. As your vision returns you see between a now prone Adrik and a cowering Ront, stands a shining Torinn with white wings spread wide. Where his metal shield once rested on his forearm, he now holds an astral shield."

"What happened?" I asked. Rubbing my head. "My axe? Where is it?" I panicked.

"Do I see the axe?" Liam questioned as he pretended to search.

"Both of you see the axe at Torinn's feet." Mr. R said.

"Torinn! Grab him!" Ront shouted.

"I dive for the axe!" Ront and I both blurted out simultaneously.

"I dive for Adrik," Torinn added.

"Torinn, give me a strength check. Adrik give me a Strength saving throw. Liam, give me a dex check."

"Twenty," Liam called out.

"Ten," I growled.

"Okay, I swear to Pelor, I'm not cheating." Daryl threw his hands up.

I leaned in to see his brown die, once again with the twenty-side up.

Mr. R blinked in amazement. "In a moment of sheer adrenaline and anger, all three of you make your moves. As Adrik makes his leap at the axe, Torinn dives at him, scooping his arm behind his back and holding him across his chest from behind. Ront, as this happens you dive towards the axe and grab it from the dirt. As you pick it up, I need you to make me a wisdom-saving throw."

"Fifteen," Liam eyed his uncle.

"You feel a slight tingle in your head. Like a hand creeping over your brain. But it quickly retreats," Mr. R depicted.

"Give it to me!" I screamed at Ront. "Give him to me!"

"Torinn, can you clear this from him?" Ront asked.

"I can try," Torinn frowned. He filed through his notes. "I cast Remove Curse on Adrik—" he stopped and reread the notes he had. "Actually, I cast it on the axe. Ront, I need to touch it please."

"What if he grabs it?" Ront asked.

"I pull him away and reach out one hand," Torinn explained.

"I hand him the handle of the axe," Ront said.

"Give me a wisdom save," Mr. R pointed to Daryl.

"Well, that's the end of my nat twenties I guess," Daryl chuckled. "But it's a seventeen. Plus nine, making it a twenty-six."

Mr. R nodded and jotted down in his notes. "Torinn, you reach out for the axe, feeling its dark presence in your hand as you grip the cold metal of the handle. It sends a chill down your back."

"By the light of Pelor," Torinn began.

"And the shadow of the Raven Queen," Ront added.

"I destroy any curse bestowed upon this weapon!" Torinn commanded.

"As you recite this spell to the axe, there's a moment of silence amidst the winds still swirling and kicking up," Mr. R narrated. "Adrik is still fighting and screaming for his axe back. And then like a caterpillar, a black crust begins to build over the axe. Creating a cocoon of what could only be described as a black tar. Torinn, your amulet begins to glow as the cocoon reaches your hand. You feel a warm energy transfer from the amulet, into your chest, up your arm, and out of your hand." Mr. R paused and took a sip of his drink. "As the energy transfers into the axe, you begin to see light breaking through the tar-like substance, cracking and shattering the crust. Adrik is beginning to calm down in your arms. You can feel the evil presence leaving the axe."

Torinn let out a sigh of relief. "It's done. The axe is cured."

"I kneel down to Adrik and ask him if he's alright," Liam directed. "How ya feelin?"

"He looks pale. His face contrasting against the thick red beard that's now drenched in sweat." Mr. R described.

I only nodded.

Liam smiled and reached his hand out for my shoulder. "Everything's gonna be okay."

The table was silent for a good minute or two. Until Mr. R broke that silence.

NEVER SAY DIE

"Boosh!" Mr. R broke in. He clicked his keyboard and a green beam appeared over the image of Faria before fading back out.

"What was that?" Rolen asked.

"I don't know, but I don't like it!" Ront growled.

"As the wind begins to die down and Lerissa falls back to the ground. Returning to her normal state. The world around you seems to grow colder. The ground begins to slowly wilt and grow black. As if all life is being drained out of the ground." Mr. R described.

"This isn't good." Lerissa sighed.

"And with that, a humanoid figure crests the horizon before you, slowly walking towards you all." Mr. R clicked again and a dark figure slowly faded in and out. Growing bigger. Coming closer. "As the figure comes more into view, you begin to make out their features. A tall, human male. Dark skin and purple eyes. Long black hair tied back behind his head."

"No," Ront mumbled under his breath.

"The male wears a long flowing robe of red that seems to drag behind him. He stops approaching you all," Mr. R paused. "Without a word, the man snaps his fingers. His hands burst into flames, followed by a bout of screams as what looks like an army crests the horizon behind the man. Each soldier dragging along one or two hostages."

"No, no, no, no," Torinn shook his head.

"Fools!" Mr. R bellowed. "You cannot kill a god!"

"No!" Ront shouted.

Mr. R chuckled that deep, ominous chuckle he always uses.

"Get out of his body!" Ront fought. "You son of a—"

"He snaps his fingers again and you watch as one of the soldiers drags forth another human male. You all recognize this man. Rugged and battle-worn, the scar across his face bringing back memories." Mr. R described.

"Bart!" I cried out.

"I will destroy all those you love!" Asmodeus boomed. "I will slaughter this entire realm! And in turn, it will destroy each and every one of you."

"I get to my feet," I interjected. "As long as we stand before you, you will never prevail!"

"Foolish," Asmodeus sighed. "In his hand," Mr. R began. "A swirl of shadow begins to form into an axe." He paused. "And the axe that once was in Torinn's hand begins to disappear into the same shadowy mist."

"Don't do this!" Ront pleaded.

"Will you take his place?" Asmodeus laughed. "Would the noble paladin of the matron of death take the place of a pathetic mortal?"

"I would take the place of a thousand mortals if it meant stopping you from spreading your evils!" Ront retorted.

"Then by all means," Asmodeus smiled. "Take his place."

"Ront," Torinn whispered. "Don't do this!"

"I must!" Ront clipped. "We need to end this once and for all! Just follow my lead." He turned to his uncle. "I get to my feet and walk towards him."

"The soldier takes Bart from his knees and throws him back with the piles of cowering Farians." Mr. R narrated. "In the group, you recognize people from your last visit. Benji and Keyleth being the prominent ones trying to keep everyone safe and calm."

"I approach Asmodeus standing as tall as I can. Staring into the eyes of Jarron," Ront explained.

"I can see the pain in your eyes as you stare into the helpless void of his eyes," Asmodeus jabbed. "Would it help you to know that I killed him slowly? It was quite painful—"

"I jam the Raven dagger under his ribs!" Ront shouted. "Twenty-seven."

"That's a hit," Mr. R nodded.

"I'm sorry my love," Ront choked out. "He's considered undead correct?"

Mr. R nodded again.

"Forty piercing damage and five points of necrotic damage." Ront sighed.

"Asmodeus lets out a cry of pain as the dagger burns in his body," Mr. R narrated. "You've killed them all!" Asmodeus shouted. "I will kill them all like sheep! Starting with you!" He snapped his fingers. "From behind you, countless numbers of kobolds, orcs, and other creatures hold you down and pin your head against the ground." Mr. R depicted.

"I charge Asmodeus!" I blurted out. "I want to run at him and leap into the air with my rage!"

"Give me an athletics check," Mr. R asked.

"Twenty-five!" I rolled.

"You charge at Asmodeus as he begins his swing," Mr. R rolled behind his screen. "And as you leap in the air you hear a familiar voice call out to you," He cleared his throat. "Adrik! Catch!" A familiar cockney accent came through.

"Benji!" I cheered.

"As you leap into the air, you see a familiar hammer soar through the air and carefully place its hilt into your hand," Mr. R described.

"Eldrith!" I whispered.

Mr. R slid me another piece of laminated paper.

Eldrith the Dwarven Thrower

Requires attunement by a Dwarf.

Speak the Command word.

You gain a +3 bonus to all attack and damage rolls while using this hammer. It has a thrown property with a close range of 20 feet and a long range of 60 feet. When an attack hits with the thrown property you gain an extra d8 of damage. The hammer returns to your hand after an attack.

Secondary attacks gain 1d10 on a hit.

"I slam Eldrith into Asmodeus!" I smiled.

"Roll me a hit," Mr. R nodded.

"Thirty-one!"

"As you catch Eldrith in the air, you turn her momentum into an arc of strength. You slam into his chest as he turns to look at you.," Mr. R rolled. "And you slam him into the dirt. Roll me damage."

"Nine damage," I rolled.

"With a crack of thunder, you lay Asmodeus into the dirt." Mr. R looked up to Torinn. "Following initiative still, that would make it your turn."

"Did we ever get the kid down from the spire?" Torinn asked.

Mr. R shook his head.

"Then I do that," Torinn said. "I get the child down and safely with Elfi and Rolen."

"You move to the spire, your astral shield protecting you from the arcs of electricity still blasting off the spire," Mr. R narrated. "You break the chains holding the child in place and move towards the large red dragon in the middle of the battlefield." He turned to Lerissa. "And that makes it your turn."

"I want to cast Feeblemind on Asmodeus," Lerissa said. "He takes twenty psychic damage and I need an intelligence saving throw!"

Mr. R rolled his dice and wrote his notes. "He's going to use one of his legendary resistances and succeed that saving throw."

"Wait! What?" Laura blurted out.

"Legendary resistance. He has a small amount of resistance where he can choose to succeed on any save. So in this case, he takes the damage, but not the effects." Mr. R explained.

"So I just wasted my only eighth level spell for him to just shrug it off?" Laura complained.

"That's what happens when you fight gods," Mr. R shrugged. He turned to Rolen and pointed to him.

"My turn?" Ben asked.

Mr. R nodded.

"I guess—" Ben clicked his tongue for a moment. "I move to Torinn and pick him and the child up."

"Is that all?" Mr. R questioned.

"That's all I can really do," Ben shrugged.

"Alright, then Gimble, you're up." Mr. R turned.

"Am I close enough to use inspiration on Adrik?" Gimble asked.

Mr. R looked at the battle map for a moment, looked at his notes, and looked back at the map. "I would say yes."

"Awesome!" Gimble smiled. He pulled up his violin and began playing an upbeat version of *The Misty Mountain theme* from The Hobbit.

"Now we're talkin'!" I laughed.

"Adrik, take one d10 inspiration," Mr. R noted.

I nodded and promptly wrote on a sticky note.

Mr. R turned to his nephew.

"I take out the item I was given from the Raven Queen on our last visit," Liam explained. He held up the piece of laminated paper from earlier.

"You reach to the now empty dagger scabbard on your belt," Mr. R began. "Wrapping your hand around the empty air, you feel a handle. From your closed hand an ethereal dagger begins to form. You pull the forming dagger from your belt. It's as black as the night. Misting with shadowy smoke off the blade."

"I drive it into his ribs right next to the Raven dagger," Liam choked out again. "Twenty-one. Does it still have sneak attack since he didn't see the dagger?"

Mr. R clicked his tongue. "I'll give it to ya."

"Forty points of piercing damage again. With six points necrotic added to it," Liam rolled.

"Asmodeus lets out a wail of pain," Mr. R said. "What is

this—this magic?" Asmodeus cries out. "You watch, Ront, as the wound begins to dissolve the bit of skin around the wounds."

"The Raven Queen sends her regards," Ront scowled.

"Send her my regards when you see her next!" Asmodeus laughed. "You watch as he points at you. The tip of his finger beginning to glow green. As a small beam of green arcane light blasts at you. I need you to make me a dexterity saving throw." Mr. R asked.

"I use evasion," Liam noted. "Twenty."

"You just manage to evade disintegration." Mr. R laughed. "As the beam of green energy blasts out from Asmodeus' finger, you dive out of the way. The beam blasting a small crater in the ground where you stood just moments before." Mr. R turned to me. "You're up."

I cleared my throat. "I would like to throw the hammer at Asmodeus." I picked up the piece of paper and read.

Speak the Command Word.

"Is there any writing on the hammer?" I asked.

"Examining it, you see a list of dwarven runes and writing scrawled down the handle," Mr. R described. "And it reads, honor, justice, glory. Long live crown Baldrick."

"I recite that out loud," I explained.

"As you read off the runes in dwarven, you begin to feel another surge of archaic power pulse through your arms. But this time it's not an evil presence. This time, you feel the warmth of another being." Mr. R narrated. "Like being wrapped in a motherly hug once again."

"I throw it," I smiled. "Twenty hits," I rolled my damage. "Thirteen bludgeoning damage."

"You wind up the throw and launch the hammer at

Asmodeus. It soars through the air and blasts him in the chest," Mr. R rolled. "He's knocked to the ground."

"Can I hit him on the return?" I asked.

"Roll the second attack." Mr. R answered.

"Twenty-six," I said. I began to roll damage. But Mr. R began narrating.

"As the hammer turns its direction and flies back towards you, it slams through the dirt where Asmodeus laid. The hammer returns to your hands." Mr. R paused. "And then the world begins to shake."

"Did we finally do it?" Rolen asked.

"No way!" Laura groaned. "If this is another life I'm going home!"

"Above the now deceased body of Asmodeus, a black rift opens in the air. And out from the rift emerges Pelor followed by the Raven Queen." Mr. R clicked his keyboard.

The battle map of Faria shifted into a painting of the six of our characters standing before the two goddesses.

"It has been done," The warm voice of Pelor broke through. "You have destroyed this evil once and for all," The Raven Queen's dry tone followed.

"I kneel before my goddess," Ront and Torinn said together.

"The planes are safer now thanks to the six of you," Pelor continued. "Our biggest mistake was granting him this power, to begin with."

"It's over," Lerissa clipped. "Why have you presented yourselves to us?"

"We have come to collect a few things," The Raven Queen answered. "You all watch as the two reach out towards the body of Asmodeus," Mr. R narrated. "And rising from the body, a small ethereal gnome, angry and fighting." he clicked his keyboard and the little gnome appeared. "And for this, we have someone who has come to see you all and help us with this nasty thing," Pelor said.

He clicked his keyboard again and another gnome appeared on the screen. This one was smiling. He wore purple and gold robes that had golden stars on it.

"Froug!" I cheered.

"Ahhh, my friends," Froug smiled. "That was my mortal name. I now go by the name Ioun."

"Wait!" Torinn gawked. "You are now Ioun?"

"Yes my dear Torinn," Froug laughed. "After I was set adrift in the astral plane, I had found Ioun's library. He bestowed upon me the responsibility of the vast knowledge of the universe so that he may once again be reborn into this world."

"So even the gods die?" Rolen asked. "Oh, and I drop my wild shape."

"Yes, we do," The Raven Queen answered. "Throughout time, we must each find a successor to take our place so that we may once again be reborn as mortals. To end our personal existence."

"The cycle of life and death does not forget any soul. Not even the gods of the cycle." Pelor continued. "It's what gives our existence purpose. So that one day we too could enjoy the closing of our time. It truly would be a curse to live forever."

"Driving one mad for power," Froug joined. "Pushing one to great lengths so that they could possibly reach a potential not meant for them. And my poor brother was one to fall upon that fate."

"What will you do with his soul?" Lerissa asked.

"As punishment for his actions in meddling with nature itself, the slaughtering of millions of innocent lives, and the attempt at domination. Asmodeus shall spend eternity in the nine hells, on the lowest level of Nessus. Where he may preside over the realm of his power. And never shall he escape this prison." The Raven Queen explained.

"So he's sentenced to eternal damnation?" Gimble asked. "Serves him right."

"And with Gimble's comments, another rift is opened in the ground. A pit of fire and screams. The gods all move their hands down and you watch as Asmodeus slowly floats down into the ninth hell." Mr. R narrated.

"So, now I presume you are also here to collect on my debt as well?" Ront sighed.

"In time, yes," The Raven Queen answered. "However, I still have a while before I will be ready to go through my rebirth." The Raven Queen said calmly. "So for now, I shall grant you a little longer in your mortal form."

"Wait! What?" Ront blurted out. "Did you just tell me that I will one day be the god of death?"

"In due time, my child," The Raven Queen nodded. "Until then, you will serve as my humble servant on this plane."

"As you wish, my Queen," Ront bowed his head.

"Now I believe there are two more who wish to visit you all," Pelor announced. "And through the rift step a recognizable figure. Dark skinned, purple eyes, long black hair—"

"Jarron!" Ront interrupted.

"Ront!" The ethereal being cheered.

"She brought you back to me!" Ront choked out through tears of joy.

But they quickly turned into tears of sorrow. His expression didn't match Ront's excitement. It was happy, but a sad happy.

"She's not going to bring you back, is she?" Ront frowned.

Jarron shook his head.

"Why?" Ront asked.

"I cannot bring every being back from my realm," The Raven Queen explained. "There are some souls that are unable to come back. And as the goddess of death, I cannot just randomly bring those back. It's very rare, the second chance we gave you."

"But I can't trade my life for his either, can I?" Ront bargained.

"I'm afraid my child," Pelor joined. "That is out of our abilities as well." Mr. R sipped his drink. "But I shall wait here for you," Jarron said. "I will wait another lifetime see you again, my love. For the day you are called to join us in the next plane."

Ront swallowed the knot in his throat and just nodded.

"I will always be here for you," Jarron assured him.

"I just kiss him," Ront cried.

"He embraces you," Mr. R narrated. "It's a weird feeling. He's there and you feel something there, but it's not the warmth and feel you remember."

Ront's lip quivered as he fought the tears that were now welling in his eyes. "I will be there soon to join you," He promised. "We will live out eternity together."

"He pulls your head up by your chin," Mr. R narrated. "Do me a favor," he asked. "Don't make my passing a big deal. Find a nice place for my ashes. Scatter them somewhere you think we would meet again."

"I know just the place," Ront smiled.

"Then this is until next time," Jarron said. "And he leaves you with one last kiss." Mr. R finished.

"Until next time," Ront sighed.

"And with that final kiss," Mr. R continued. "Jarron turns to the goddesses and the three of them walk into the rift." Mr. R turned to me. "Adrik, there's one more thing," Froug said. "There's one more visitor who's come to see you all."

"Who?" I raised my eyebrow.

Mr. R clicked his keyboard and on the screen in front of Froug, a purple feathered bear appeared.

"Gerbo!" I cheered. "Hey, buddy! I run up and give him a huge hug around his neck!"

"You charge at the owlbear who in return trots at you and nuzzles into your hug," Mr. R narrated. "He rolls into you and over you. Rolling in the dirt hugging and wrestling each other."

"Is he like the others?" I asked. "Like, ghosty-like?"

"From what you feel," Mr. R paused. "Gerbo is as real as anything."

"Oh, I missed you buddy!" I laughed.

"Adrik, can I ask a favor of you?" Froug asked.

"Anythin'," I blurted out.

"Gerbo needs open space and adventure in his life," Froug sighed. "And as the god of knowledge and keeper of the library of Ioun, I can't provide for him like I used to."

"What're you tryin' to say?" I questioned.

"Will you take care of my good friend?" Froug smiled.

"Are you serious?" I exclaimed. "Of course I will!"

"I thought so," Froug smiled. "He's been very patient with me in wandering the library day after day. I just feel bad that he isn't getting the care he needs, following me around."

"I will make sure he's well played with and taken care of for you!" I assured Froug. "You can count on me—count on us." I corrected.

"I thought so," He smiled. "Well then, I guess this is another until next time."

"Until next time, my friend!" I replied.

"Froug nods and smiles at you," Mr. R narrated. "Gerbo realizes what's happening and tries to leave with him." He chuckled. "No buddy," Froug sighed. "I need you to stay here with Adrik. He will take care of you. He will love you as much as I do. Maybe even more."

"I walk up next to Gerbo and scratch the top of his head," I said.

"You hear Gerbo whimper," Mr. R frowned. "It's a sad sound. It's that distinctive mix of owl and bear. But the emotion behind the noise says a thousand words."

"It'll be okay, buddy," I assured Gerbo. "We will love you! We'll feed you well! And most importantly we can run and play all you like!"

"And I will make sure to visit every chance I get!" Froug promised. "He steps up to the owlbear one last time, wraps his arms around Gerbo's neck and gives him a big squeeze!" Mr. R depicted. "With tear-filled eyes, Froug mouths the words 'thank you' and turns into the rift. With a swallowing sound, the portal closes. Leaving you six and Gerbo in the midst of a destroyed Faria. The townspeople begin to move out into the open. Their faces distraught and confused."

"Well," Gimble shrugged. "We've got some work to do!"

ENDINGS AND BEGINNINGS

"As the next few months pass," Mr. R began. "The six of you stick around to help rebuild the town. Adrik, between you and Gerbo you have nearly rebuilt every building in Faria. Helping lift each fallen wall into place, carrying supplies with the town miners from the mountains and doing a lot of the heavy work in the town."

"We wouldn't have it any other way!" I smiled.

"Lerissa, Torinn, and Rolen," Mr. R pointed to each of them. "Rolen, you helped the farmers regrow most of the lost crops before the winter months come through and freeze the ground. And as a little added help, you brought life to the vegetation. Giving the town color and life once again."

"It's the least I can do," Rolen said modestly.

"Lerissa, you helped restore the Grand Myastan Library. Even incorporating the library that Froug left behind. You and the keeper of the library, Chareeve Myastan, build a teleportation circle in the library. Giving people access to across the world into Froug's Library."

"Now that's how it should be," Lerissa laughed.

"Torinn, you found a home on the hill that sits under the mountains to the south. Inside the hill, you found and restored the ancient temple of Pelor. A temple that dated back to just after the pilgrimage of the fey beings and the fall of Oculous. A monument erected by the late paladin Randal Dundragon."

"Can I expand the temple?" Torinn asked. "Make it a universal temple? One that pays homage to the Raven Queen and Ioun as well?"

"What if we made a monument to Ioun in his own library?" Lerissa suggested. "Since he's the god of knowledge and whatnot."

"I could live with that," Torinn agreed. "Then I would like to expand the temple to the Raven Queen as well, with Ront's help of course."

Ront nodded in agreement.

"Alright," Mr. R said. "You and Ront spend the next few months restoring the temple. Erecting new monuments to the Raven Queen to stand beside her sister's statues and shrines." He took more notes. "Gimble and Ront," he pointed to the last two. "In the rebuilding process, and with the help from Draven's guild, you both manage to restructure their economy. Helping them reorganize their councils and businesses." he chuckled to himself. "And Draven recovered his wagon from the middle of the trail. Using it as an opportunity to move his guild headquarters in the backroom of the Dragon's Tale. Taking over Reita's rooms."

"Really?" Gimble questioned. "I understand Ront being in politics. But I'm just a bard. I'm not political."

"No," Ront smiled. "But you sure as heck can negotiate."

"What're you talking about?" Gimble raised his eyebrow.

"I throw an arm over his shoulder," Ront explained. "I can't do this without you. Don't worry, they won't make you do anything. They just need to be organized."

"Fine," Gimble agreed. "But only if you buy me a drink at the Dragon's Tale later. I hear Keyleth is playing tonight and I want to be there when she needs a violin." he laughed.

"Deal!" Ront nodded.

They both smiled at each other. That unspoken understanding of the joke.

"Is there anything else any of you want to add to your story?" Mr. R asked looking around the table.

Rolen raised his hand. "What about Elfi and the child?"

"Ah yes," Mr. R remembered. "Well, what happened between the two of you?"

Ben's eyes grew wide with panic. "I-I get to decide that?"

"Unless you don't want to—"

"No!" Ben blurted out. He pursed his lips for a second. Rolled a couple times. Thought a little longer. "After the events that destroyed the town, I relocated these two into a small house off to the outskirts of Faria. Elfi and I are raising the child together. Until we find his home. I train him in the ways of the druids and nature. I also built Elfi her own observatory slash library so she can once again continue the work of her late mentor."

"Wow," Lerissa shrugged. "I guess you really are husband material."

"That's just being a decent human being. I don't know what's so hard about that." Rolen sighed. "But anyways, I set her up for a lifetime of accomplishment and knowledge. Like any wizard should have."

Mr. R nodded and jotted some notes.

"After everything is built and we've finally come to the time where we rest, I want to find Benji," I explained.

"Oi!" Mr. R laughed. "Adrik, 'ow've ya been?" Benji asked.

"Benji!" I cheered. "I pull him into a dwarven hug."

"You both slam into each other, followed by a tight squeeze," Mr. R narrated. "Wha' brings you aroun' to the Dragon's Tale?" Benji asked.

"I wanted to return this to you." I pulled out the laminated piece of paper from my binder and handed it to Mr. R.

"Oh," Benji smiled. "Eldrith. You kept 'er."

"Ever since the battle. She saved our lives. You saved our lives!" I reminded him.

"I merely 'elped out a fellow Baldrick!" Benji slammed his chest.

I copied the gesture with a smile.

"But I can't accept 'er from ya," Benji said. "She is meant to protect the crown. An' who better to protect than a literal Baldrick!"

"That's too much, Benji," I declined. "I couldn't take her from you. You two have been through everything!"

"Adrik, I'll let ya in on a li'l secret," Benji whispered.

I leaned closer to hear him.

"I'm ol'!" He shouted in my ear. "I don't need no reason to use 'er again. An' someday soon, I'm gonna pass along like e'ryone does. An' what will become of me beloved 'ammer then?"

"But Benji—"

"No buts," Benji raised his hand to cut me off. "You are the next leader of the Baldrick clan!" He set his hand on my shoulder. "An' it would be me 'onor if you wielded Eldrith high in the glory of our people!"

I looked down at the piece of laminated paper and spun it around in my fingers. "I couldn't tell you how much that means to me, Benji. I will bring her back to the mountain where her glory will shed across our people once again!"

"Then me work 'ere is done," Benji sighed. "Now, 'ow bout a drink?"

"I couldn't say no to that!" I agreed. "It's on me."

"You 'eard the man, Bart," Benji laughed. "It's on the lad!"

"I want to eventually join them in the tavern," Rolen added.

"Me too!" Gimble and Ront blurted out.

"I guess I should, too," Lerissa laughed.

"Count me in as well," Torinn joined.

"You all make your way to the tavern. Joining each other in drinks. The entire tavern eventually comes to life as it begins to get later in the afternoon." Mr. R clicked his keyboard.

It was a familiar painting that appeared on the screen. One we hadn't seen in quite some time. The Dragon's Tale was in all its glory. The torches and fireplace illuminated the smiling faces at every table. The wall behind the bar littered with kegs of all shapes, sizes, and colors.

Mr. R clicked a second time and a lute began to play over the sounds of chatter and conversation.

"Oh click that one more time, Matt," Jacob smiled. "I hop on that stage and join Keyleth!"

"Amidst the laughter and drinks you six share, you all watch as Gimble's ears perk up at the sound of a lute. Without skipping a beat," Mr. R clicked. "He runs to the sound and begins to play alongside her."

The sound of violin and lute together in a jig got my foot tapping and my adrenaline kicking.

"Lerissa," I looked at her. "Would you like to dance?"

Lerissa smiled. She picked up her drink and downed what was left. Wiped away the residue from her lips and nodded. "What the hell! There's no one out there who wants to kill us for no reason!"

"Huzzah!" Ront, Rolen, and Torinn cheered. They smashed their cans together with a clank.

"I grab Elfi's hand and follow Adrik and Lerissa," Rolen added.

"You grab her hand," Mr. R began. "She hesitates for a moment. But realizes what your plan is. With a smile and a chuckle, she obliges and runs into the crowd with you."

"Here's to living for another day," Torinn raised his glass to Ront.

"Here's to seeing another sun!" Ront replied.

The slammed their cans together again.

"As the night grows older and you all begin to grow tired, you find your ways to your respective homes to sleep off the alcohol and entertainment." Mr. R narrated. "The merriment of the town rings throughout the night. Echoing in the valley." He rolled. "But something else begins to echo through the night air."

"No!" Ront groaned. "We defeated the lich! We bartered with gods! We've battled so many people! What more does this world want from us?"

"The ground begins to rumble," Mr. R continued.

"I light the warning fires of the temple!" Torinn explained.

"The sound of stampeding feet grows closer to the town."

"I grab Adrik and Gerbo and race them to the streets to face whatever is coming!" Rolen directed.

"We're already out there, waiting!" I explained.

"I watch from my tower in the library, spell book ready!" Lerissa said.

"I carefully climb out of Keyleth's bed—" Gimble began.

"Ooo!" Laura teased.

"And head into the streets as well!"

"As you all rush into defense mode. Accompanied by Benji, Bart, and Keyleth," Mr. R began. "The stampede gets louder and louder. The ground begins to rumble and shake. It feels like a small earthquake. Not enough to damage, but enough to scare." Mr. R rolled his dice. "And bursting from out of the darkness of night, a swarm of frog creatures charges through the city, paying no mind to those in the streets, merely running around you to get to their destination."

"Frogs?" Torinn questioned.

"As bullywugs, grungs, firenewts, and a few slaads barrel past you. You notice they're not here for the town. They are running around the town to reach the lake on the other side." Mr. R explained. "After a good twenty minutes of the world-shaking under your feet, it falls silent. And for a moment of pure peace in the world, it's almost unsettling."

"But well needed," Rolen smiled.

"After an awkward amount of silence, it's broken by an eruption of croaks that ring through the valley." Mr. R clicked his keyboard and the room rumbled with frogs croaking.

"This is the most peculiar ritual I've ever heard of," Mr. R said in a familiar female's voice.

"Wait until I tell you about the human traditions of Midwinter," Rolen laughed. "You'll love it!"

"In a stir and commotion, you all attempt to make your way back into your homes once again." Mr. R smiled. It was that ominous smile.

He quickly clicked the keyboard and an ear-splitting roar rang through the house.

"You're all interrupted by the frighteningly familiar roar."

"You're kidding?" I asked.

Mr. R didn't say a word.

"The Tarrasque!" Torinn complained.

"All the way out here?" Rolen groaned.

Mr. R chuckled. "And that's where we will end tonight's game."

UNTIL NEXT TIME

WE ALL LET OUT A COLLECTIVE GROAN.

"You're really gonna do us like that?" Jake asked.

Mr. R just laughed. "I think it's due time you all had a challenge." He leaned back and folded his arms.

"What?" Ben blurted out. "A challenge?"

"Uncle Matt," Liam joined. "We've been chasing the same evil lich for months!"

"And you defeated him easily," Mr. R replied.

"Easily might be grossly oversimplifying it," Laura argued. "We had the right gear, but that was no easy feat!"

"Well, next week may end up a challenge," Mr. R shrugged. "Or it might mean we need to do another campaign if this is too easy for you guys. We'll just have to see."

"You're insane, old man!" Liam claimed.

"That may be," Mr. R laughed. "But you come from the same gene pool, my friend."

"O villain, villain, smiling, damned villain," Daryl recited.

"Ooo Hamlet! Nice," Jake reached his fist out and Daryl promptly bumped it with his own.

"To thine own self-be true, And it must follow, as the night the day, Thou canst not then be false to any man," Mr. R recited back.

"Oh and right back at him with the famous parental advice from the father of the year, Polonius!" Laura called out.

"It looks like we have a nerd-off, ladies and gentlemen!" Ben joined in.

"Do you bite your thumb at us, sir?" Mr. R continued to recite.

"Is the law of our side if I say 'ay'?" Daryl returned.

"Wow, this is getting good," I said.

"I think we should cut this off before they break into a full monologue," Jake shook his head, smiling. "I know you both too well, and unless we nip this now, it's going to be six more hours of iambic pentameter."

"And what's wrong with that?" Daryl asked sarcastically.

"I didn't say it was a bad thing—" Jake tried to get out.

But Daryl cut him off, "Out of my sight! Thou dost infect my eyes!"

"Now you've done it!" Jake jumped from his chair and ran at his brother, who had already leaped from his seat and run towards the kitchen.

"Help! He's gonna kill me!" Daryl laughed as they ran through the house.

"I guess we should call it there, then," Mr. R joked.

I pulled out my phone to check the time.

2:53

I could feel the weight of my eyes as I stared at my phone. Like I'd been beaten with the Sandman's sandbag. I didn't want to move or anything.

And then my phone started to buzz.

<u>Mom</u>

-When do you plan on being home?

-Soon hopefully. We just ended.
-Trying to avoid a Shakespeare fight.
-Love you!

-Let me guess, Matt and Daryl?

-Bingo!

-Stop them before they start biting thumbs!

-You're too late.
-Jake's chasing Daryl already.

-Those boys are gonna break something again
-I just know it
-Anyways, text me when you head home!

-Yes Ma'am

-Love you kiddo

-Love you too!

I put my phone on the table and began packing my stuff. I could hear Jake and Daryl in the front room. And by the sounds of the bargaining and pleading, Daryl was in a headlock.

"Should we let them figure it out on their own?" Liam asked.

"No, this was my fault," Mr. R sighed. "I'd better go save Daryl before his brother causes him to pee himself."

"No don't, stop, don't do it." Ben pleaded sarcastically.

But Mr. R ignored it and wheeled out of the room.

When I turned back around to finish packing my bag, I heard a clicking noise followed by the familiar startup chime of a Nintendo DS. I perked up to see who it was.

Sitting with a smug smile on his face was Liam, hiding behind his small screen.

"I thought that would get your attention," he chuckled. "You got a game in ya?"

"Well," I returned the smug grin. "I didn't bring mine with me. Didn't want to get burnt out before the Smash Bros tournament next week."

"But one game," Liam whined.

"Sorry bud," I shrugged. "It's not with me. There's not much more I can do."

"Buzzkill," Liam mumbled.

"The one and only," I smiled.

Liam got out of his chair and sauntered into the kitchen. I knew that was an upset for him. But really, I wanted to surprise him at the tournament. I'd been training for a while now so that I could actually have a chance this time around. Usually, I go to these tournaments with Liam and Daryl, just to get eliminated in the first round. But Mom and I have been playing nonstop for weeks now in preparation for this tournament. I don't plan on winning. I just want to be able to move on past round two!

"So, does he not know?" I heard Ben ask.

"Nope," I laughed. "I want it to be a surprise. I'm really hoping that I get to play him early so that I have a shot at kicking his butt!"

"Well, I think you've got a decent chance!" Ben assured me. "And I hope you can kick his butt, too!"

"Thanks," I smiled. "Are you guys coming too?"

"I'm not," Ben sighed. "I told your mom I'd pick up the extra work since you guys are out. Plus that gives me a couple extra bucks to go waste at the card shop. They got in a new set of foil cards and I want to see if I can't get my hands on one or two of them."

"Nice," I answered. "Did they say whether it's a mixed set? Or is it another land set?"

"I think Josh was saying they might get some planeswalker foils. But most definitely a majority of land cards."

"Dang," I shrugged. "Text me when you find out though. I really could use a better planeswalker. I just can't seem to get any of my Ajani cards to win. I think I should use a black deck now. White just isn't my thing I guess."

"That's all the fun of the game," Ben laughed. "Learning

what does and doesn't work. I've been through more decks that didn't work than I have that meld well. It's all about experimentation!"

"I thought it was all about beating the other player," I joked.

"What's the point if you're not trying new things?" Ben asked. Totally missing my joke.

"Never mind," I shook my head.

"He's clueless," Laura cut in. "He wouldn't know his left from his right if Mom didn't sew an L on his sleeve when he was younger."

"She did not!" Ben glared at her.

"And who's to say I'm lying?" Laura smirked. "It's my word against yours."

Ben pursed his lips in anger. He grabbed his bag off the chair in front of him and stormed out of the room, mumbling to himself.

"You really are his sister, aren't you?" I laughed.

"What makes you say that?" She asked. She moved her hands frantically across her body as if she was trying to find something. "Is my stupid showing?"

I couldn't help but giggle at that.

"I guess I can't say that he gets it from me," She sighed.

"Hey now, that's not true!" I blurted out.

"So you agree he's dumb, too?"

"What? Wait, no," I stuttered. "Where's Admiral Ackbar when you need him?"

"Oh, so now you think I tricked you?" Laura squinted.

"W-what? N-no! Never!" I continued to blabber out.

"Jack," She smiled. "I'm just messing with you."

I sat there for a moment, not quite sure how to process the next thing to say.

"You alright there?" She asked me. "You look like you blew a gasket or something. You're not gonna die on me again, are you?"

I shook myself back to reality. "No, I'm good. I was just lost in your—in my thoughts." I caught myself, hoping she didn't.

But she did. She always did. She was too smart for me and I knew it the minute she smiled. It was that kind of smile that melted you. Opened you up like an Easter egg.

She snapped her fingers in my face. "Seriously, you're starting to worry me. You zone out in the midst of talking to me. Is there something wrong with me?"

"N-nothing's wrong with you!" I blurted out. "You're perfect in every way!"

"Oh, well thank you," She laughed, sarcastically tossing her hair over her shoulders.

I could feel the blood racing through my body. "Hey Laura," I said, out of nowhere.

"That's my name," She answered.

I will be one hundred and ten percent honest, I have no idea what I'm doing or saying. It's literally just spewing from my mouth.

"W-would you like to maybe go, and, I don't know,"

Don't do it! You can't survive the humiliation if she shoots you down! You're insane!

"Maybe wanna go catch a movie sometime?"

That's it! My life is over! I can never leave my house again. I can't come back and play anymore. My life is forever tarnished because I can't control my p's and q's!

She's eyeing me now. Like she's squaring me up to fight.

"On one condition," She smiled again.

I could feel the cold sweat trickling down my neck. My mouth was becoming so dry I could feel my tongue cracking. The blood in my body raced between my face and my nether regions. This became way more awkward than it needed to be.

I quickly nodded, trying to ignore the fact I was physically showing everywhere!

"I get to buy half the night," She demanded. "Either I buy the movie and popcorn, or I get to buy dinner. It's your pick. But I get to pay for half the evening. Sound like a deal?"

"Deal!" I blurted out. I hadn't even thought about dinner. Then again, I wasn't planning on asking her out on a date.

"Great, text me then, when you want to do this thing," She leaned down and kissed my cheek. "You know my schedule and where I'll be during the week if you need me." She stood back up and walked out the room.

I sat there in the game room silent. I had finally done it. I finally have a date with my dream girl! And I didn't die trying to ask her out! Does this mean I'm finally a man? I thought that was when I had a bar mitzvah.

Who cares? I'm going on a date with Laura! What's Mom gonna say? I'm going to have to talk to her mom when I pick her up! Should I bring her flowers? And what's Ben going to say?

Oh man, I didn't even think about Ben! He's gonna kill me!

I spun around to head into the kitchen. When something hit the back of my head. I turned back to see what hit me. From around my neck, the camera that'd been hanging there since we took our break, fell to my chest.

I examined it for a moment. I picked it up in my hands and turned it on. I clicked through the pictures on the SD card.

There were the pictures I took tonight. Each person smiling and having a great time.

I clicked on the only other picture on the card.

It was Mom and Dad! They were no older than I am now. Mom was looking at the camera smiling while dad kissed her cheek. It'd been years since I'd seen my parents together like that. I couldn't even tell you if they'd ever actually kissed each other because I was too little to remember.

But this picture was them. I had that feeling that they were both sitting right in front of me. In fact, they kind of were. This was taken at one of their game nights. You could see the dice and character sheets scattered across the table behind them. The same table my dice were scattered across right now. The same table, just missing the tv screen in the middle of it.

And they were sitting on the same side I sit. The only real difference was the room they were in. It wasn't Mr. R's game room. At least, not the one I'm standing in now. This was the original game room! The one in Mr. R's parents' basement. His original Batcave. And it was as glorious as the current one.

The picture spoke to me on a level I can't explain. Just seeing my parents happy and together again filled me with happiness and warmth.

I looked up from my camera at the room I stood in. The shelves of games. Cabinets of miniature statues. The table specifically designed for our weekly hang out and game sessions. This room was my second home, where I lived with my family. And I don't think I could ever be happier anywhere else.

"I'm telling you! He's going to agree with me so don't even bother asking him!" I heard Liam arguing in the next room over.

I threw all my stuff in my bag, picked up the box of Aunt Marisha's things and headed into the kitchen. But I was stopped in the doorway by a bickering Liam and Daryl.

"Tell him I'm right, Jack!" Liam shouted in my face.

"No, tell him he's an idiot!" Daryl argued back.

"Well," I shrugged. "Technically you're both idiots and most likely you're both wrong. But what are you fighting over?"

"This dimwit thinks Link is the best fighter in Smash Bros!" Liam explained.

"And he thinks it's Samus!" Daryl added on.

"So I was correct?" I laughed.

"What?" The both turned and looked at me stunned.

"It's no wonder you guys never win these tournaments," I shook my head. "Everyone knows Kirby is the real MVP."

"That pink ball of a black hole?" Daryl tried piecing together.

"Yeah, that pink ball," I responded.

"Something is wrong with you!" Liam blurted out. "Maybe we're both wrong, D, but I think Jack's lost his freakin' mind!"

"They might need to lock you in an institution," Daryl joked.

"That might be," I smiled. "But you never said I was wrong."

"I—" Liam tried. But he realized I was right. Again.

I shook my head and laughed at them, pushing my way into the kitchen with my things.

"You look like you're ready to get going," Jake said as I stepped into the kitchen.

"You know how my mom gets," I answered. "She's already freakin' out."

"She's just wanting to make sure you make it home," Jake told me. "And also not dead in a ditch or something."

"Only when the clown finally comes out from the sewer," I joked with him. "Until then, I think I'll be fine."

"Well, be careful and drive safe. Okay?" Jake raised his eyebrows.

I nodded and gave him a salute.

He returned the salute.

I turned and made my way to the front door with my things. But was stopped by a voice.

"Jack! Hold up a sec!"

I turned around to see Mr. R coming from the kitchen.

"I thought I missed you," He said. "I wanted to give you this."

He handed me a manila envelope that was folded into a smaller rectangle.

"I want you to give this to your mom," He instructed me. "And you're not allowed to open it!"

I nodded.

"No," He shook his head. "I need you to promise me that you won't open this. It's for your mom only!"

"I promise!" I assured him.

"Good," He smiled. "Now I'll let you go. Your mom's probably having a panic attack."

"I wouldn't doubt it," I laughed. I turned to head out the door, but I stopped and turned back to Mr. R. "Hey, Mr. R."

"Yeah?" He answered.

"I just wanted to say thank you."

"What for?" He asked.

"Everything you've done for us. Especially me and my mom," I explained. "Everything you've done for us since and before Dad was gone. I think if he was still around he would still be as proud to call you his best friend as he was all those years ago!"

I could see he was fighting back tears.

I moved in and gave him a tight hug.

"You're so much like him. In every way, kiddo," He whispered in my ear. "Don't ever lose that. Okay?"

"Never in my life!" I assured him.

"Thank you for being such an awesome kid!" he choked out. He patted my head before letting me go. "Now seriously, get out of here! Your mom has probably called the cops twelve times!"

I smiled, turned out the door, and waved goodbye.

I unlocked my car and hopped in. It was definitely much colder outside. Enough that my car struggled to get started. But it finally kicked in with a loud roar.

I pulled my phone out and tapped the Spotify app. Scrolled through my playlist down to the bottom. I clicked on the song *Goodbye Blue Sky* by Pink Floyd. I sat and listened to the beginning ambiance of the blowing wind.

Then I moved to open the envelope that Mr. R gave me. I know he said not to. But I mean you can't give someone a mysterious envelope and not expect them to peek.

"Look, mummy," The little British girl said over my car speakers. "There's an aeroplane in the sky."

The guitar cut in as I slipped the top off the envelope.

I reached in and pulled out a stack of cash. And when I say stack, I mean stack. It barely fit in my hand! I put my hand back in and left the money in it. I pulled out the other contents inside. It was a letter.

. . .

Jack,

I knew you would open this even after I told you not to. That was my intent with being very specific with it. You are truly your Mother's child.

I want you to keep this money. It's not mine, to begin with. This is every single dollar you mother and father ever gave me for anything. Pizza, booze, games, the whole nine yards of everything. I have saved this with the intentions of one day giving it all back to them. And I finally get that chance.

I want you to take all this money... And put it in a timed bank account that I've already set up for you. They'll explain it to you. But you're not allowed to take anything from it until your 18th birthday!

From there it's all yours. Do what you choose with it. (Hopefully, pay for college. That shit's expensive!) But the choice is yours! Do what you will with it!

You're an amazing kid with a bright future
-Matt

P.S. Let your mom in on this secret, please.

I sat there for a moment trying to understand what just happened. Not only has Mr. R been an amazing person in my life. But he's been secretly saving my parents' money for me to have a future with!

He's set me up for life. And we were never aware of it!

I couldn't stop the tears as they poured from my eyes.

I cleared them the best I could, put my car in drive, and headed home to share the news with Mom.

Her baby boy was going to have a good future, thanks to her and my dad!

We were going to be okay, thanks to my Dungeon Master Matt Rollins!

ABOUT THE AUTHOR

Raised on a healthy diet of geek and pop culture, Antony has come to share his love and appreciation for role playing games and geek culture. If it's random comic book facts, Star Wars obsession, or just the measly obscure movie reference, Antony is there!